INSIDE MY HAT

AND OTHER HEADS

by

Alun Buffry
Jacqui Malkin
Melissa Doordaughter AKA Ariadne Snail
Steve Cook
Winston Matthews
Sarah Dougan AKA Sarah Sativa
Rocky van de Benderskum
Phil Monk

Inside My Hat and Other Heads

Published by ABeFree Publishing December 10 2019
ABeFreePublishing@yahoo.com

ISBN 098-1-9163107-0-4

Authors and Artists:
Alun Buffry
Jacqui Malkin
Melissa Doordaughter AKA Ariadne Snail
Steve Cook
Winston Matthews
Sarah Dougan AKA Sarah Sativa
Rocky van de Benderskum
Phil Monk

CONTENTS

Cover designed by
Matt Maguire, Candescent Press
https://candescentpress.co.uk/coverdesign.php

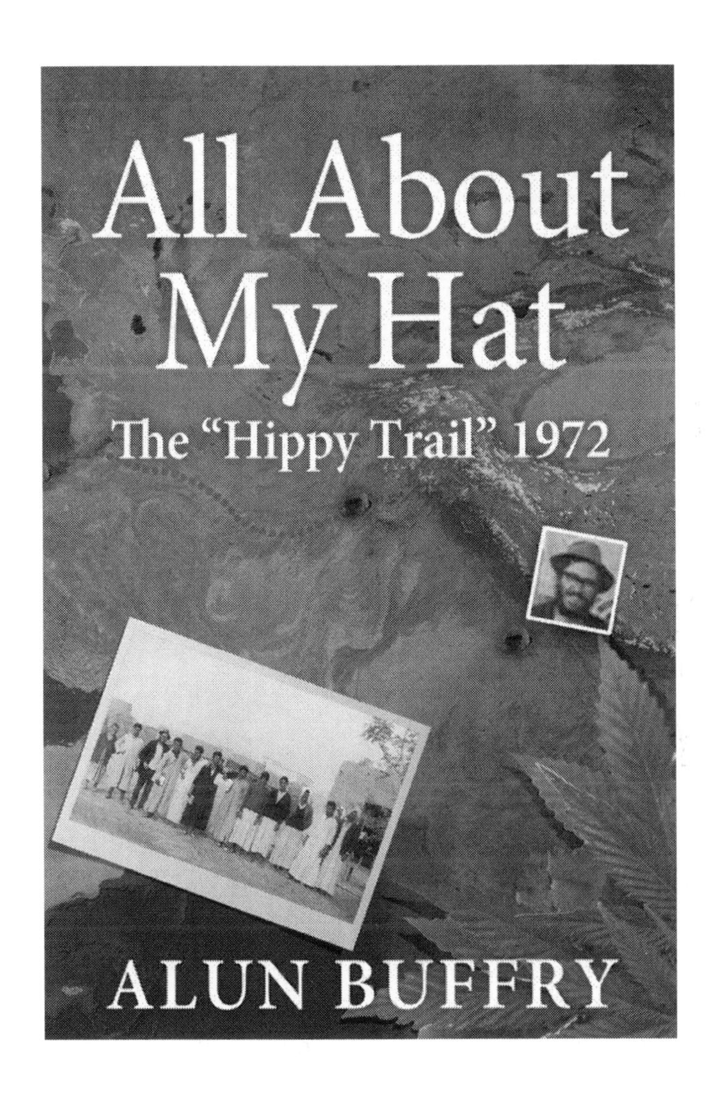
All About
My Hat
The "Hippy Trail" 1972
ALUN BUFFRY

SOME POEMS

By

Alun Buffry

Alun graduated in Chemistry at UEA in 1971and then travelled overland to India, a journey which he says changed his outlook on life. Since then, he has devoted much of his life to fighting for Human Rights. In 1991, he was imprisoned for ten years for conspiracy to import and supply cannabis. In 1999, several years after his release, he co-founded and registered the Legalise Cannabis Alliance (LCA) as a political party in thee UK, standing for election to Parliament in Norwich in 2001. He is the author of books and poems including:
From Dot to Cleopatra, A History of Ancient Egypt
All About My Hat, The Hippy Trail 1971
Time for Cannabis, The Prison Years, 1991 to 1995
Out of Joint, 20 years of campaigning for cannabis
Damage and Humanity in Custody
Myhat in Egypt, Through the Eyes of a God
The Effie Enigma, The Motherless Mothers

AS THE MIND FLIES SO THE BIRD WALKS TO THE MOUNTAIN, OR ZEN AND THE ART OF BEING (LAZY) (A POSTCARD FROM KATHMANDU)

Today, outside, the weather is hazy.
Stayed in all day, feeling quite lazy.
Where to go now, we often talk,
Then decide it's too far to walk.

Two hours there and two hours back,
"Let's stay here, and have a snack".
Just fifteen minutes up to Baba's.
and we know that there, food's better by far,

But here we eat, for our stomachs sake,
whatever's available as it's no effort to make.
"Well", I say, "I guess that's what
a holiday's for on a day that's hot."

"We're free, we don't have to do anything.
We can fly like a bird with a broken wing."
"How can that be, such a bird can't fly?"
"We can't do much either and here is why-

Cos - cor it's hot outside today,
and "wherever we go we have to pay",
or "My leg's aching, stiff and weak,
and there's nothing in the bazaar we seek."

"Stomach queasy, or head aching?
Let's be another chillum a-making."
Then, "Let's go in a boat!"
"No, don't want to row!"

Or, "Let's climb that mountain, look at the snow!"
Oh, if only we could get up there and back,
Without having to walk on that mountain track.
If you close your eyes and lay on your bed,
you can go anywhere inside your head.
If you know how to master the Traveller's Trick,
You'll be there in an instant
and come back so quick.

Pokhara, Nepal

H

Transparent butterflies flit amongst the transient stars
as bouncing bubbles burst on broken moonbeams.
Rainbows run around the rippling rivers
fumbling over faithful fountains.
Sparkling shadows seep between the sunsets
whilst whistling weepers wave from windows.
Many millions mourners make a martyr,
standing somewhere silently beyond space.
Loosely rhyming lines of lullabies
gag the gorgeous gems of galaxies,
never noticing the numbered nomads,
driving dozens dromedaries down deserts,
purposely persuading passers by to pay,
countless crispy notes and coded coins -
before the beautiful beholder is belittled.
Frequently the foolish faulty fiddlers
only offer ornamental oodles,
very vaguely valued vibrants,
ever aiming for an endless evening,
questioning the qualities of quanta.
Yet the yellow yodellers yearn
as all the armadillos answer
zealous zebras zimmering in zoos.
It's intelligence involving inhibition,
exalting in exciting extras ever.
And all the world is in an atom - H.

THE CELL

The cell was cold, dark, empty and bare.
The walls screamed to themselves - there was nobody there.
The bars in the window stood firmly and strongly.
The cell was alone, rightly or wrongly.

The door to the cell was locked up tight.
It stayed that way all day and all night.
No-one came in to this lonely cell,
To make sure the walls and the windows were well.

The cell, itself, was just doing it's time.
It could have been your cell, or even mine.
It waited the years just doing it's best,
Wanting for little, but a prisoner guest.

One day, the door was opened, by a man with a key.
Even then this one cell never really felt free.
The warder looked in, said "Is all OK?"
Slammed the door shut and just went away.

But this cell was so lucky, if only it knew,
For amongst so many it was one of a few.
For thousands of others were imprisoning men,
Bleeding their hearts out, again and again

The cell next door, which was much the same,
One man inside it, I forget his name.
One night the cell door was finally banged.
Next morning the man was found to be hanged.

GOD'S GAME

Left Marrakesh today, to Fez, but on the way,
Felt a lacking of some sort - forgotten my passport!
Got off the bus again, cursing my damned brain,
Went back to where we'd stayed. God's little game was
played.

Amidst all this god-dam fuss, in little Hotel 'Mus',
I got the passport back! But my head's about to crack!
It's started now to rain. I think I'll catch the train.
'Cos lover must be there and I wish I was with her!

Not possible this time, to use the railway line.
So I sit in sorrow, waiting for tomorrow,
When I hope that I can go, if rain don't turn to snow.
Well the money goes so quick, I'm gonna have a fit,

I want to smoke some stuff and call the devil's bluff.
Illusions all around, and my head aches from the sound
Of rains and cars and mules and stupid tourist fools.

But writing down these lines has made me feel quite fine.
It's just that I couldn't half do with along hot bath,
And get rid of the dirt, and wash my only shirt,
And jeans and socks and all, and go and have a ball,
In Fez.

RAM RAM BUSES
(India 1985)

From Delhi on an Indian Tourist bus,
We left thinking they'd take care of us.
An Indian video humbly plays and we're
Told in 24 hours we'll reach Kashmir.

The journey goes into the darkest night,
As jungle and hills slowly dodge our sight,
The road now is just long and straight,
No bumps and bends or jerks to hate.

We're speeding along, ever so fast,
As if this journey is our last,
The road the driver's trying to keep,
Me - I'm just trying to fall asleep.

Suddenly, we swerve, a crash, a jolt,
Us thrown around, bus comes to a halt,
We look through windows only to see,
We hit a small tractor and just missed a tree!

Spite driver's brave efforts to curve and sway,
One side of the bus has been torn right away!
Amidst cries of Oh God!" - in Hindi "Ram Ram",
And in my own mind "Oh shit, oh damn!"

No one here seems able to tell,
Whether we're earthly or in heaven or hell.
But nobody's hurt, so we all get out,
A policeman a sweeper's given a clout.

For without thought he's just learned that he'd officially signed
A statement unread because he was blind.
There's nothing to do now but sit and wait,
Arriving Kashmir we know we'll be late.

Then mosquitoes surround us and all rush in,
"There's three dozen humans in a half open tin!"
They must have shouted and told their friends,
"We can buzz all about them and insanity send!"

Well I know it's our blood they are trying to drink,
And "Kill the bastards" is what I think,
And now the sun has gotten bright,
People are gathering to smile at our site.

Apparently the tractor driver was drunk,
The cop wanted baksheesh or he'd be sunk.
Ah, now they're trying the bus to fix
With hammers, wires and broken sticks!

It'll be midnight tomorrow before we arrive,
If just 36 hours more we can somehow survive.
But surprise, surprise we weren't there all day,
For two hours later we were on our way.

RIVER ALIVE!

Whether we laugh, or whether we cry,
the river of life goes rushing by,
down the hills and mountain sides,
into valleys, long and wide,
towards the ocean that is its goal,
its journey travelled by our soul.

When I was but a little boy,
the river rippled and dashed with joy,
and as I grew and longed to learn,
the river for the ocean yearned.

As young man travelled round the world,
the river twisted, turned and twirled,
eager to find its resting place,
eager to travel in time and space.

And as the seeking man grew older,
the river found the bigger boulders,
but on it travelled without care,
it knew its destiny's not there.

The rushing water's now quite slow,
the river old has nothing to show,
it's happiness is calm and deep,
as old man takes his final sleep.

The ocean that is never ending,
is to the sky its waters lending,
to rain again on mountain top,
to make sure life's rivers never stop.

The river's message lies in this
ocean of Mercy, Peace and Bliss.

MONKEY ON THE BENCH

We looked up, at the bench, and there sat a Monkey;
Scratching it's head as if trying to understand.
"Why is there so much crime, throughout my sad land?"
The Prosecutor said, "These men here are Evil!".
The Monkey nodded it's head, as if to agree.
"Why should Monkey let evil men free?"

The Defence Lawyer, he said, "I concede naiveté!"
The men in the dock just looked on confused.
The Laws of the Courtroom are daily abused.
"We need more time to convict them." said the Beast in Blue
"It we hunt hard," he said, "we might find us a case,
To lock them away in utter disgrace"
The men, you see, had God's Herb Seed taken,
And grew a fine crop of the peaceful Weed.
A crime without victims, yet men won't be freed.

WAITING FOR HABIB

(Kashmir 1981)

The kids in the village of Aru,
Had eyes fixed on us both like glue,
Their eyes shining, open wide,
As they're sitting side by side.

Their granny's there, old, toothless and bent.
Her happy life is almost spent.
But still, just now and once a while
She looked at us and gave a smile.

Whatever it was they were trying to say,
We never knew before on our way.
Their hospitality ever so warm,
Amidst those mountains tall and calm.

We waited for three hours and more
Before Habib's donkey man we saw,
Then off we strode with just a wave,
To walk and eat and sleep and rave.

For Roxana, Musaka a place called home.
For us it was a stepping stone.

MAN, PUT IT RIGHT YOURSELF

Look down for a moment at this Human race,
From origins to now, changes we trace,
That 'though most of the time we didn't want war,
We let politicians and military men store
Our weapons of hate - or protection they say,
In case we have enemies to strike at one day.
So, now we all stand facing each other,
Knowing all die if man strikes his brother.
Some people here shout about nuclear power;
The atoms are split not to make enemies cower;
Used instead to make heat, movement and light,
But some people feel radiation ain't right.
The burns, they tell us, will start with an itch,
Yet daily we continue to push down the switch,
For the sake of economy and to ease our lives,
To amuse the children and appease the wives.
None of us want deadly fumes in our heads,
Yet most of our cars are still pumping out lead,
And carbon monoxide and satanic gases
Which surround the globe and will choke the masses.
See - we all need to travel and warm up our homes.
It's so far from us that strange ozone.
The scientists, we hope, the solution will find,
While we run round like mad men to satisfy our minds.
We hide away the old, the mental, the spastics,
We dig our big holes and fill them with plastics,
We flush down the toilet with all kinds of shit,
Polluting the rivers and oceans with it.
The fish, they are dying, some species are lost,
We all say we're sorry but won't pay the cost;
Won't give up our luxuries, take care how we tread,
On this our planet, and live gently instead.
There up the road is a chemical factory,
The products, we think, are quite satisfactory.
The pollution it's causes around us, us bugs,

But it's all in the creation of bottles of drugs,
To cure all (they say) of illness and sores,
Forgetting to tell us the factory's the cause.
Ask how can we stop it, make the guilty atone,
When we are all using the same economics at home?
So, next time you notice the rivers all stink,
Remember at home what you put down the sink.
Next time that you feel that the air is impure,
Remember the fumes and the smoke that we pour,
Out of our chimneys and cars.
Think of the mammals!
Remember each one of us is in essence an animal.
And if you choose now not to swim in the sea,
Remember the nasties we put there by thee.
One thing we all know in our heads is for sure,
A Huge sacrifice is needed and maybe much more.
We must think of the things that we use and we trash,
What we burn and destroy will have a backlash:
Poisoned air, water and radiation kill slow,
And the poor Human race has nowhere to go.
Unless each person can get into their head,
That the cause and effect will make it all dead.

GOOD TO SEE YOU AGAIN

Two thousand years ago, a child was born.
A king He was, a Crown he should have worn.
Yet in a humble stable, in amongst the beasts,
Wise men and shepherds bowed
their heads unto His feet.

The child, He grew and travelled forth to learn,
To find and teach the Secret that we yearn,
And Master took from men disciples few,
Though many more would follow if they only knew.

So Master's all-too-short life had to end,
Disciples had to struggle for their lives to mend,
Through faith and hope, they tried not to stray,
From Master's unsophisticated way.

Then men had visions onto paper that they wrote,
Along with Master's words and stories that He spoke,
So me, religious, later read about that wondrous age,
When God Almighty manifested as a sage.

Alas, the words, though, all had double-meanings,
The Truth is not quite always as it's seeming,
And in 2000 years divisions grew,
Of those who thought, had Faith, and those who knew.

If Master only came to us but once, it is a shame,
For men in ignorance need to see Him once again.
Besides the stories of the manger and the crèche,
We need to see The Master in the flesh!

JAISALMER

Jaisalmer, oh Jaisalmer!
Not a lot of hassle here.
Just cows walking in the streets,
Adding smells to earthly heat,
Makes us want to drink more chai,
But "No milk!" the people cry.
All those cows yet still no milk,
All those shops that just sell silk,
Desert life's just not the same,
Camels struggling, what a shame,
To let us climb upon their backs
And if they moan they know the crack.
Driver up there perched on top
Passing songs until we stop
At water hole or shady tree
To eat a precious chapatti
Made by the men, full of pride,
Over fires with veggies fried,
In spices which do not have names,
But we don't care 'cos we have pains,
In legs and arms and even feet
From riding camels in this heat.
Three days the desert journeyed on,
We listened to the Rajputs' songs,
Passing temples, villages
Passed to us through ages.
Suddenly, the words we hear:
"See over there, sweet Jaisalmer!"

LOOKING FOR NEW YEAR

Kathmandu: morning mist, disappears, mountain view...

Clouds spreading, sun shines, sky turns sea-less blue.

Magic palace on the hill, silver morning light,

As the haze clears away, giving city sights.

Street below slowly wakes, dogs with horns and bells

All the homeless people there, washing at the wells.

Today is Nepalese New Year, should be celebrations,

Where they are is not too clear, to our mild frustration.

Maybe dancing in the street, or are there parades?

No-one here seems able to tell, where New Year's Day is made.

Life goes on as usual, everywhere you glance,

New Year doesn't seem like here, the spirit to enhance.

Where would we go in England,

If New Year we were there?

Down a pub or round a house

Or down Trafalgar Square?

I guess that from outside, it'd look all much the same,

Like we don't celebrate New Year, they'd think it was a shame.

So maybe here in Nepal, because I cannot see,

There's celebrations all around, invisible to me.

Katmandu

DIVISION

In this world, division

Makes one desire decision,

As if one were almighty God

Seeing all through mindless fog,

As if the choice we make is ours

To pick or simply smell the flowers,

Whether left or right to turn,

Whether to sleep, rest, play or learn.

Why can't we see that we are His,

He breathes,

He thinks

He moves

He lives.

IN THE BELLY OF THE BEAST OF BABYLON

They bin trying to curb
The free use of the 'erb
They don't give 'em no bail,
They just sling 'em in jail.
In the Belly of the Beast of Babylon

And dem people they's a-crying
And all a-wondering why-ing
No drug, no harm, no pain,
And then there be no gain,
In the Belly of the Beast of Babylon

Law won't let 'em people's high.
Them there makes them famlies cry,
And the years are gonna pass,
For 'erb smokers there on mass,
In the Belly of the Beast of Babylon

Them there law-abiding judges,
That bear all freedom people grudges,
They gonna rest so calm at night?
When they know them people's fright?
In the Belly of the Beast of Babylon

NINE MONTHS

After nine months a baby was born,
And it's name was hate and its heart was torn,
Never to be seen a smile on a face,
Of men waiting so long in this goddam place.

God help the world if it only knew
What hate would become if it ever grew
Into an adult and then got free
To destroy all, believe you me.

For after the beasts had had their way,
Lied and deceived to lock men away,
The Magistrates fine all turned their blind eyes,
Whilst inside at night the chaplains all cried.

Month after month they stay on remand,
Listen in mystery to conspired bad plans,
Never allowed just one word in defence,
The law in this country just don't make much sense.

So locked up these men at country's expense,
Guilty or innocent they sit on a fence,
Awaiting the trials on some distant days,
When men either walk free or get thrown away.

After nine months inside, away from the sky,
The birds and the trees and the friendships that die,
the children, the lovers, the life that won't wait,
Innocent and guilty share hearts full of hate.

LIFE ARE I

EYE – the dot;

Hi – the cot;

My – and not;

Why? – so hot?

Try – the pot!

Tie – the know;

Lie – the plot?

Cry – the blot!

Sigh! – so what?

Nigh – the sot;

Die – forgot;

Bye! – the clot;

Eye – the dot;

Hi – the cot!

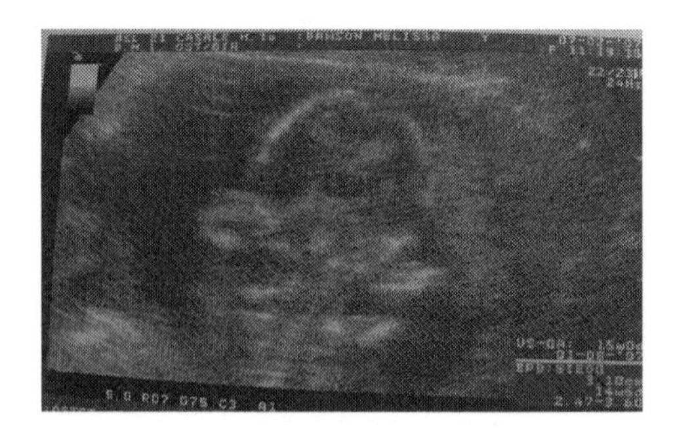

SAND THROUGH THE HAND

Life flows so quick like golden sand
Each grain a day passed through god's hand
Each moment precious as a jewel
And Yet I waste it like a fool.

You looked at me my heart to sway
But blind I was and looked away
Back to desires and lust and greed
From which You begged me to be freed.

I never ceased to grab and hoard,
Always forgetting my sweet Lord,
That Love lives on within inside
From whom no soul would wish to hide.

I pray to you Lord, to be so kind
And give me strength to ignore my mind,
So from your path I'll never stray
And at your feet my life will stay.

Those things for which once I craved
You showed inside and I was saved,
Life's flow became a flow of bliss.
Each grain a chance Your Feet to kiss.

And if ever I stray again,
Please call me back to Holy Name
That Light inside me, make it glow,
Your endless love, please let me know.

WIND IN THE PILLOWS

Life's not always as it's dreaming,
With endless videos streaming,
When friends decide to stay,
In dreams, but on the way.
Will I wake up from this seeming?
With starving children screaming,
As half-full plates of food pass by
Parents have to watch their children die;
Whilst all we do is pray!
Reality seems just a noisy fart away.

It must be worth a try to mend
A fracture with a dreaming friend.
'Cos parting makes on cry,
We ask the hidden reason why.
People, places, faces without meaning,
Souls so many sleeping dreaming,
Faces that are smiling sad,
Intent is good, result is bad.
They tried to make my head dismay,
But is reality but just a noisy fart away?

The dreaming woke me, made me cry,
To Life from which we're meant to die,
In communes without meaning –
Not always what they're seeming!
But all inside my body's head –
I'm really sleeping in my bed!
The world around, the words, the sounds,
I wake to face another day.
Reality was just a noisy fart away!

POSITIVITY

Always to be found in this the same place,
Throughout our universe of time and space,
On I will travel, at my own pace,
Can you now see it, in my face?

Never to question how or why,
Upon this earth I find I,
Content and amazed beneath earth's sky,
Yet soaring above white clouds on high.

Hidden within us there is a clue.
It looks like I, it looks like you
For once we were one and that is true,
Now one of so many amongst quite a few.

There is a Love, there is a Light,
Forget any guilt, ignore any fright,
Focus within on a wondrous sight,
The future is now and it's ever so Bright.

WICKLEWOOD

They're watching from the corn field there,
I heard the signs, the smoke within the air,
Not illusions all in Buddha's many minds,
They watch us 'cos they know we're not their kind.

See there - the Wicklewood, the road beyond,
Just secreted besides the Olde Ducking Pond,
A car, a scar, on landscape's flaw,
Soon we heard the knocking on the door.

They came, they grinned, they even knew our names.
They played their endless searching games,
Seeking for a tiny lump of hash -
Who'd have though the law so crass.

WAKING IN NEPAL

Outside is a cloudy sky, bright sun in between, a slight
breeze, the sound of one man chanting, and all,
somewhere else, a few notes, occasionally, of some type
of flute, a strangely musical cacophony of bells and horns
and clattering.

No two horns seem to sound the same!

A motor engine sounds like a tractor, probably a bus.
Beep, beep, beep.

As I look out through the window, I see tin rooftops,
Bhimsen tower, a glorious white erection against the blue
sky.

And there a temple, a pagoda, and a woman with washing
laid out to dry; pigeons, crows, people attending to potted
plants in their roof-top gardens; below a bicycle rickshaw.

A cow, a man with a bundle of wood on his back - a
cockerel crows, a motor bike, three men trying to move a
fridge, a young girl with proud breasts sitting, staring into
space; a kid rolling a wheel amongst the rubble whilst
other kids look on admiringly.

Yet another dog, a tempo (three-wheeler), two boys hand-
in-hand, a goat.

Cocks crow, horns, bells into the far away mountains'
quiet peace.

Monkey Temple like a magic palace on the hill, behind,
another hill.

Shame about the dusty haze.

INSIDE THESE WALLS

Can't stand it! Can't stand it! No more at all!
In a Universe so big, I'm alone and so small.
Can't stand it no more, inside these four walls,
For Love that is limited is no love at all.

There's no-one to see, to hear or to smell,
No-one to whom my story to tell;
Somewhere is Heaven but this sure is hell,
Crying alone in apathetic small cell.

I reach out through letters I send out each day,
Searching for Love in a written-down way,
Not knowing in here how long I will stay,
There's no sitting quietly and no running away.

The walls are so solid and lifeless and thick,
The world outside is terribly sick,
Sleep passes the time, please let it pass quick,
Put a smile on the face, and let the clocks tick.
I'll stand it! I'll stand it! And the day will come,
When the time I've spent here will be over and done,
And the walls will collapse and then who will have won?
Who'll see how much life inside is devoid of fun?

The prison breeds hate for the judge and the key
The man so upright and pathetically free
Won't open his heart and my door and me free,
Back to the world of hate that I see.

But who can stand it? I know not of any,
In company daily of sad faces so many,
Split from their lives-loves and all until when
Their sentences pass and conspiracy ends.

Can't stand it! I'll stand it and on I will go,
And where it will take me, I really don't know,
As society insists on it's pathetic law-shows,
To lock up the people who just want to glow.

DREAMS

Dreams rapidly vanish
into the murk of physical realities.
Truth along rings in the
Eternal now again.

Distant past, distant dreams,
fade slowly into the void.

Why can't words be spoken softly,
as of old?

Here and Now,
memories, dreams, sadness, regret, hope,
disappointment and despair,
all cease to exist.
It is the Only place to be.

MIRHLEFT

Mirhleft by the Sea,
A nice little rest for me;
A place to sit for a while,
Watch the Donkeys single file,
Walking up and down the street,
Poor creates have no shoes on feet.

And I wonder why those men,
Walk up the street and back again,
Maybe it's to look at me,
Watching them whilst drinking tea,
Sitting outside the small café,
Passing through the time of day.

A SPRING COLD

How cold you've gone since Spring.
Is this the time that you begin
To play your guessing games?
But not those games for me,
If you care really, to be free.

I've realised my lucky lot
Is put away on the shelf on top,
Sitting to ignore the pain
Coagulating in my foggy brain.
Over, under, inside out,
Speak your mind but please don't shout.

I'm not too young to fall and die.
You're far too young to sit and cry.
Raspberry and cold-shoulder pie,
The custard's for some other guy.

A PRAYER

Do I have to go today, Lord?
Why won't you let me stay, Lord?
Or do I have free will?

Where can I head for now, Lord?
I don't even know quite how, Lord;
Without your Divine Will.

Oh show yourself to me, Lord,
Before a catch the bus, Lord,
If it be your will.

I know that you are here, Lord.
I feel you in the air, Lord.
Everywhere you fill.

PRAYING FOR THE BUS

We left Delhi 4 PM today,
To Kathmandu by bus,
At midnight whilst still on the way,
We stopped without a fuss.

It had been quite a bumpy ride
Through places without names,
The seating wasn't very wide,
No sleep was such a shame.

Half a day upon the bus we are,
Frying in the heat,
This is no de-lux bus by far,
It is a lying cheat.

Another bus is coming here.
Well, that is what we're told.
Exactly when is not made clear.
No Indian's that bold.

Then still we're waiting on the bus,
Later on that day,
A Foreign girl invited us,
To come along and pray.

"We'll do some prayers and puja chants,
"And maybe sing a song,
"It that don't work we'll do a dance,
"And bus will come along."

The bus to Kathmandu, we think,
Will much improve our mood,
And on the way, perhaps a drink,
And then a plate of food.

"Oh bus, oh bus, show us your magic,
"Come and save our day,
Our journey now is feeling tragic!"
"Oh, now we're on our way!"

RECURRING ILLNESS

1.. I'd thought I'd been lucky to get out of Afghanistan alive. I had been ill for months and now, after a three day bus journey from Kabul, I found myself sitting in the street. My head was spinning and I could hardly walk. I had been vomiting again throughout the night and unable to keep even water down for long. I was dehydrated again and I still had little money. Nobody seemed to want to help for a while, then a man asked me if I needed help. After telling him I was English and wanted to get to the Embassy, he helped me to the busy and dusty street corner and pointed me down another street filled with various vehicles and people, saying that it was the American Embassy. I slowly walked to the entrance and discovered it was in fact the UK Embassy after all. Then I remembered I was in Tehran, on my way home. The Embassy was closed and the costumed guard at first would not let me in, but I insisted, entered a large room and lay out on wooden bench, saying that is was UK and I would stay until I saw an official. That is how I was taken to the Tehran hospital. I was treated well over the week of my stay, put back on my feet and afterwards the Embassy guy took me back to my hotel to get my bags and next day took me to the airport from where I flew to Heathrow. Unfortunately, just as in the previous two hospitals they did not cure me.

2...TRANSLATION: the dirty hippy man that Mahatma Ji brought into my Chai shop by the bridge in Haridwar, did not look well. He was hot and I think he had been smoking charas. We did not speak the same language but I wanted to help him and I wanted to tell him to go to a doctor. I could only give him Chai with extra sugar and milk. Then he soon went off and I never saw him another time.

3. It wasn't until I had reached Delhi by train that I knew that I was far more ill than I'd thought. As well as having dysentery, I had contracted Hepatitis A, the infectious sort, that I thought I had picked up in Kabul. I spent a week in hospital in Delhi, well fed and resting in the cool, which was good for me as I had completely run out of money. It was good that I had left Haridwar which was where I'd first got sick. I don't think there would have been much of a hospital there and surely no ashram would want me

4. I had a horribly-tasting porridge for breakfast that morning, along with poorly cooked eggs and toast and tea. That was the day I became ill with dysentery, the day everything changed. That day I was cleansed.

5. Kabul was a lovely city with friendly yet strange people and hardly a local woman to be seen without a full Burkha. But it was filthy. They had little care for hygiene. The water provided on the tables of restaurants was dodgy; even bottled water could not be guaranteed clean and often may have been from the tap. Whilst salads were washed in tap water, fruit was not washed at all. We saw donkeys shitting in the street next to open stalls cooking and selling

food, fruit or bread. We were advised to be careful when eating with a wet fork or spoon or when drinking in a cafe, for fear of hepatitis or other sicknesses. As for the opium den, well it was the pits. We had two pipes and left hoping that we would not be ill later. It was nothing like the clean opium farm we had stayed at for three days in Iran.

6. When I was admitted into the hospital in Wales, they took away my Iranian medication and ignored my diet of no fried food or salads. As a vegetarian, then, I had to eat salad and chips twice a day until their test results came in, after which time they reinstated my diet and fed me better. They kept me there one week and loaded me up with pills. Apparently I had a bacteria that came from dirty water.

7. The bus ride from Kabul to Tehran took 5 days, changing buses several times, sleeping and eating in the cheapest places I could find, having to drink tap water. I got sick a few times but I did arrive in Tehran, dirty, hungry and ill.

8. TRANSLATION: We were sitting in the shade of a holy tree and smoking chillums of the holy herb, when I saw a thin and bedraggled western man with long hair walking besides the Holy River Ganges. I watched as he slowly stepped down into the rushing waters and he disappeared beneath them briefly. After he had pulled himself out and was walking closer, I called to him to come to us and invited him to smoke with us, the Holy Herb. I asked him why he had come to the city of Haridwar and he said to

meet with me. We laughed; we shared a drink of water from the river. A short while later he left with Mahatma Ji from the ashram of Prem Nagar, the place of the Guru Sant Ji Maharaj, I never saw the young Western man again.

9. I sipped fruit juice on my way back to the railway station bench where I had slept. I think it was that what made me puke. I'd been quite stoned on chillums that day so being sick was doubly unpleasant.

10, I saw a young man with very long hair sitting in a busy street in my home town of Tehran. He looked as he needed help so I spoke to him. He asked me to show him to the UK Embassy. I knew it was round the corner in the other big street so I took him there. It was in fact UK embassy so I left him there and he went inside. I don't know more than that.

11. After several chillums besides the Ganges and a brief dip, I met a Mahatma and was invited to stay at an ashram. I drank some tea and returned to my sleeping bench at the train station in Haridwar. I became sick and never made it to the ashram. The illness was to last for weeks and reoccur. I have often wondered if it was something I drank or just Karma.

12..Peshawar was one of the filthiest places I had to stay in. Eating almost anything was a risk. We were lucky to be taken to The Secret Restaurant, run by Swiss hippies, which was clean with good food and dope. Our hotel was dirty with an open toilet on the roof. There were a lot of sick people in Peshawar.

13. The Mahatma took me to a chai house and ordered a cup for me. He invited me to join the Arti parade through Haridwar early evening and said that afterwards, if I wished, I could go and stay in the ashram. He left without paying for the chai, telling the waiter that it was baksheesh and not to ask me to pay. The waiter or tea-house owner did not seem to happy with that. The chai tasted strange but it was hot day so I drank it down fast. Afterwards I went back to the bench at the railway station where I had spent the previous night, I thought to relax until the evening parade. On the way I bought some fruit juice and sweet cakes. It was not long afterwards that I began to vomit and soon I had diarrhoea so I never made it to the Ashram.

14. TRANSLATION: I was walking alongside the river with a group of Premies on our way back to our ashram. A local Baba called to me and there I met the young man from UK. As were many young men who visited our city, he was long-haired and quite dirty. We took him to a Chai shop where I ordered a drink of chai for him, telling that he should not be charged any money. The owner was not pleased but served chai. I invited him to join our Arti parade that evening and to stay at our ashram. Then we left. I never saw that young man again.

15. I'd awoken early and took a breakfast of spicy chai, porridge and eggs on toast. I wasn't too keen on the porridge; it was slimy and too sweet. Then I made my way across the bridge to the other side of

the Ganges, one of the major holy rivers of India. It is said that to drink the waters of the Ganges is to purify the soul. So I strolled along the river bank and spotted a group of younger men sitting around an orange-robbed elder – they called them Baba's or holy men Sadhus and they smoked chillums of hashish dedicated to the god Shiva. He shouted and waved me over. On such a hot day, sitting in the shade of the tree smoking a chillum was appealing enough, alongside a possible dip in the river. So I went over and sat with them. They lit and passed me a chillum. I gave a couple of rupees and we smoked another. I said my thanks and carried on walking down besides the river but soon was invited to smoke another chillum with a different group. By now, I was very high. I took a quick dip in the Ganges but slipped my footing and quickly found myself below the rapidly moving water, getting a mouthful. By luck or grace, I managed to pull myself out and clamber up the steps. I was soon sipping weak fruit juice with another Baba, smoking more chillums. This Baba asked me why I had come to Haridwar. "To meet you," I said and we both laughed loudly. He asked if I would like chai and said that soon the Mahatma would pass by and take me for tea. After drinking a strange tasting chai I went back to the station to rest on my bench, intending to accept the Mahatma's invitation to his ashram. Then I got sick. I puked onto the station platform and managed to get then to the toilet where I emptied my bowels. It was the beginning and the end – the beginning of an illness and end to my outwards journey. Maybe it was a cleaning?

16. TRANSLATION: I am the Station Master at Haridwar; the Young man from England had slept on the platform bench. In the morning he left. He came back again late that afternoon and returned to the bench. I decided to let him rest there. After a while I saw him being sick over the platform onto the tracks and then he rushed into the latrine. That was at the end of my working day, so I went home and prayed for him. The God never showed me that man again; I do not know what happened to him. The sickness here can quickly kill people from the West.

17. My position is Security Guard at the British Embassy in Tehran. The young hippy man was stretched out on a bench in Reception at the Embassy when I arrived. Although the Embassy was closed that day, he had, I was told, insisted that he be allowed inside as it was UK territory and he was British. He was quite correct. He told me his name and explained that he was travelling back from India after becoming ill there with dysentery and hepatitis of the infectious kind; he did look very ill. He told me that he had been in hospital in Delhi and in Kabul. He had run out of money but some had been sent to the British Embassy in Kabul, but instead of using it to fly back to the UK, he had left most of it at the Embassy and tried to go all the way by road. So he had been several days travelling and had booked in at a Tehran hotel. That morning he had set off to the American Express offices where he hoped would be some money waiting for him. I decided to take him direct to the Tehran general hospital where they admitted him immediately; then I made arrangements to transport him to the hotel to collect his baggage

and then to the airport to fly back to Heathrow, one week later. I know that is what happened but apart from that, I don't know. We get quite a few poor travellers coming from India or Afghanistan with little money and poor health, that need help to get home. In this case it was the man's parents that paid; often it is the country itself, then we must take their passports when they arrive back in the UK until they repay the repatriation costs.

18. I was staying at the same hotel in Kabul. He got more and more ill. I know he was being sick a lot, getting dehydrated and hardly eating. Then one day I heard that he had been taken to the hospital and they kept him there for about a week. I was still at the hotel when he got back. He still wasn't very well, but able to walk; when they took him in, he could hardly stand up. A lot of people get sick on their journey through Iran, Afghanistan, Pakistan, India and Nepal. I must be one of the lucky ones.

19. Inside the opium farmer's house was surprisingly clean and comfortable. It was all ground level, cushions and carpets and low tables, sleeping mattresses on the floor. The village was very basic, just a small group of stone houses, a rough road running through it, where we had driven to the house. Quite a lot of donkeys were tied up outside. Soon after we arrived, they served us black tea with sweet cakes, followed by bread, salads and dips, all of which we ate with our washed hands. That was quite novel, no forks or spoons, but somehow it seemed so natural. The water, they said, was good to drink as it came from the well. After lunch we lazed around

chatting for a few hours, then our host, the opium farmer's son, invited us to smoke opium. Apparently the father had permission from the government to grow the poppies and, strangely, was not only a supplier of opium to locals (and maybe the occasional travellers), but he was also the local policeman. We smoked several pipes each: we were each given our own mouthpiece that slipped easily onto our end of the long wooden pipe with the bowl at the other end; as we inhaled to maximum, the farmer applied heat to a small ball of black opium with he turned, gleefully, until he knew we could inhale no more. Actually, although not one that I intended to repeat, it was a pleasant feeling, a relaxed, dreamy buzz, in the room with the men who were also laying on cushions, taking their turns, was nothing at all as I would have imagined an opium den to be. I felt safe.

20. The train ride from Delhi to Haridwar took many hours. The carriages were crowded and dirty and the stink from the non-flushable toilet was sickening. I had very little money left so ate what was available at the many stations where we stopped. Dahl and chapatti or samosas, spicy milky sweet Chai and biscuits or sweet cakes, lots of bottled water although I wondered if they were simply refilled from a tap. It was a very uncomfortable journey and as soon as I reached Haridwar and was off the train with the crowds wandering off to do whatever they do, I spotted a bench on the platform and stretched out and slept for the first time in 48 hours. Mercifully, nobody disturbed me or robbed me. Next morning I bought a cheap breakfast and headed off to cross the River Ganges.

21..I am an English girl, 21 years old and have travelled for a while around India with a boyfriend, but we had split up. One early evening, I was wandering about New Delhi with little purpose and no money, when I spotted Al sitting on a wall. He was long-haired and bearded and looked friendly enough, smiling as I approached him. I introduced myself and he invited me to sit besides him. I explained that I had come to India over a year ago with my boyfriend but when I got pregnant, he left; I told Al that I'd had an abortion and was now penniless and hungry. He told me that he had been ill with hepatitis A and dysentery and that he had been in hospital in Delhi. Well he did look quite ill, very skinny and worn. He said he was just 22 and I was just 20. Al said that he could not give me money but I was welcome to share his fat-free meal at the Chinese restaurant and that he was sitting waiting for it to open up. That evening and for many weeks to come, we shared food. That night we lay together in the local park but he would not get close as he said he did not want to risk giving me hepatitis. After a few days he received a few pounds from England; about a week's wage there but should last many weeks here. Al wanted to get back to the UK overland and he agreed to take me with him. Actually, I just wanted to get to Kabul. We took the train to Amritsar then buses through Pakistan to Islamabad and Rawalpindi. They were two cities, new and old, right next to each other. We stayed in a cheap hotel in Rawalpindi. The hotel was as dirty as the streets. I had to take a bus to the new city of Islamabad to the British Embassy to pick up some money that my parents had sent. Then we took buses to Peshawar and then through the

Khyber Pass to Kabul. The money went quick though. We'd been in Kabul a week or so and he started getting sick again. One day he couldn't stand up so I took him to the hospital and they kept him there. I visited after a few days and he looked so much better but he did not know when they planned to release him. I got the taxi driver to translate and he said that the only doctor that spoke English was away until the weekend, so they were keeping Al 'til then. Al said that they were feeding him on soggy rice and black tea. He came back to our hotel a few days later. He was not happy when I told him I had given most of the money away to a French woman whose husband was locked in the prison, and I had lost my passport. Al wanted to leave Kabul as soon as he could and said he thought he'd die there if he stayed. So he helped me get a new passport and himself went to the embassy for help. He managed to get some money from his parents sent out. But when I got the new passport they wanted me to have to go back through the Khyber Pass to the border to get an entry stamp, or they would not let me out of Afghanistan. That was stupid, to me, to have to pay for two bus rides when I thought they should be able to do it in the post. We argued about that a lot. We had a weird trip on acid then, which seemed to bring us closer together but we still argued the next day. Al said that if I would not go to get the entry stamp, he would catch the bus alone to go west. I didn't really care as I was not going back. So one night he said that the next morning he would either go back to the border with me or go west alone. I decided to stay. Al gave me half his money and left. I never saw him again.

22. My job is ward orderly in New Delhi hospital. Sometimes we have to care for sick Europeans, Sometimes they have no money or are drug addicts. This young man from the UK was admitted to the ward. It was clear he was very ill; he was very thin with long hair and had no money. But I could also see he was not a drug addict. I made friends with him and helped him by giving him extra food, dahl, vegetables and chapatti. He was in the hospital for about a week, then released although I knew he was still ill. I remember his name was Al and he often wore a Fedora hat.

23. Al was in hospital in Delhi with no money, according to the phone call. My job the Embassy was to visit people in that situation to see how we could help. They did seem to be looking after him well but he had no money for when he left the hospital. I loaned him ten pounds

PCP - PHENCYCLIDINE 2, 7, 11

It was the summer of 1971. Zed and Ben had recently graduated in chemistry and were sharing a room in an apartment and trying to save money to travel. They were both 21 years of age.

After returning from a drinking session in the local pub, they shared a couple of joints and Ben produced a glass phial containing a clear liquid.

Zed asked what it was.

"PCP. Phencyclidine. They use it to make Angel Dust. It's a trip," said Ben.

Well, although Zed was quite drunk, he wasn't going to simply swallow an unknown liquid of unknown strength at midnight.

So he asked Ben where he got it and how many trips were in the phial.

"I don't know," said Ben, "I got if from Denny. She gave it to me to keep safe because her husband is in hospital. He made it. He's OK though, just took too much!"

"Wow, fuck, I'm not sure about that. Let's have a look," said Zed.

Ben handed the phial to Zed who opened and warily

took a sniff.

"It's carbon tetrachloride," said Zed, "I'm not drinking that.

"I reckon it's dissolved in it 'cos PCP may not be soluble in water. So if we pour it onto hot water it may evaporate off and the trips will be in the water or maybe crystallize out."

"Yeah, OK, let's do it."

Denny was actually married to the chemist that had made the drug but she was also having a relationship with Ben. On occasion Zed simply went out for hours so that Ben could enjoy his time with her. Denny was not with them at that time though.

Having performed the experiment, they did indeed see crystals forming on the top of the water which they had put in a glass tumbler.

Ben suggested that they dip cigarette papers in to collect the crystals, as he said it was like LSD in blotting paper, but they did not have blotting paper. As Ben dipped a paper, Zed saw him lick his fingers. Another paper, another lick.

"Stop licking your fingers!" he said.

Soon Ben had placed six papers to dry out.

"I think we should drink the rest," he said.

"Well I guess most of it must be on the papers," said Zed.

"I'll get some orange juice and we'll drink half each."

Zed went to the kitchen and came back with a bottle of orange squash and a second glass. He poured half the solution from the one glass to the other, added some squash and stirred it with a pencil.

He picked up his half0glass and swallowed half of it.

Ben picked up his own half glass and swallowed the lot. Then, without warning, he drained Zed's glass too.

Listening to some Jimi Hendrix on the stereo, Zed decided to write down his experiences on this substance and found himself a pen and notebook. Then he sat back, closed his eyes, listened to the music and floated away.

It wasn't long before Zen heard Ben moaning. He opened his eyes to see Ben laying on his back on the mattress on the floor, waving his arms around and frothing at the mouth. Needless to say, Zed panicked and started to wonder whether the same thing was about to happen to him.

So he grabbed his notebook and looked for his pen; the pen was nowhere to be seen. All there was handy was a yellow-inked pen. So he picked up his yellow pen and wrote in his notebook.

"Ben is laying on the floor frothing at the mouth and waving his arms around, Foxey, Foxey Lady."

Hendrix was still playing on the stereo.

Zed wrote nothing about what they had consumed or how much of it.

It wasn't long before Zed realised that Ben needed help but Zed was in no position to give it. It all became very real for him.

Zed by now was becoming very confused about what was actually happening and what was happening in his brain; he was becoming increasingly concerned that he may end up semi-conscious, like Ben. In fact, Ben looked unconscious now. Hendrix stopped singing and Zed put the record back to the beginning (it was vinyl in those days).

Zed decided to go upstairs and wake up Chris, whom he trusted.

As he started to climb the wooden stairs they changed into large stone steps, with plants and creepers down the wall, which was now like the face of a cliff. To his other side there was a long drop to the valley below. It was not so easy climbing the stone steps as they kept moving, but he made it to the top where there was a massive rough wooden door with magical symbols carved into it; stars, moons, pyramids. He banged loudly on the door, as one would do with a door that size.

Moments later the door opened and Zed saw Gandalf, or some other wizard, dressed in a dark blue gown with stars and moons on it. The wizard looked dishevelled and displeased. "What you banging for?" he asked.

It was at that point that Zed remembered he was actually upstairs in the apartment, talking to Chris, who was wearing his dressing gown and had just got out of bed. Zed realised that in fact he had been banging on the bedroom door, rather loudly. There was no massive wooden door, no symbols carved on it, no creeping plants and no cliff.

He explained the problem with Ben, to Chris, but Chris seemed drunk and did not seem to fully understand what Zed was saying. Nevertheless, Chris followed Zed downstairs. As soon as he saw Ben, Chris suggested phoning a doctor. He told Zed to go out to the phone box and dial his doctor, whose number was 271127, while he, Chris, stayed with Ben.

Zed had no problem with that and the doctor, a woman, said she would be there as soon as she could.

By the time Zed got back home, the doctor was pulling up outside in her car. She went in to see Ben and straight away asked what he had eaten and drank; had he attempted suicide?

Zed was not keen on telling her that they had both taken PCP but wanted to tell her also that he was sure that Ben had not tried to kill himself. So he told her they had been drinking a lot of beer and that Ben had taken some sort of drug. She seemed happy with that but said she would have to call an ambulance. She left the apartment and returned a while later. It was not long before the ambulance turned up. They carried Ben to the ambulance and told Zed he could go along; they were taking Ben to a local hospital to pump out the contents of his stomach.

Zed was not keen on that, but agreed and went along. He noticed that the ambulance crew had numbers on their lapels. One was number 11 and the other was number 27.

Zed himself was experiencing both the outer world, which was looking very strange and magical, and the inner world which was filled with images and ideas. He felt as if he was thinking on several levels, and existing on several more. He remembered the number on the apartment was 7.

When they arrived at the hospital, they carried Ben on a stretcher to the inside to a ward and put him on a bed behind a screen. Zed was told to wait at the other end of this very large room. He could see a nurse and one of the ambulance drivers chatting down by the screened bed. They were laughing, probably flirting, he thought. Yet when he looked closer they appeared quite grotesque, their faces and bodies misshapen; they sounded as if cackling now, like witches at a cauldron.

Soon the nurse came over to Zed; she looked OK

again now, and was smiling. She told Zed that Ben was to be stomach-pumped to remove the poisons. After that, she said, Zed could go with his friend when they took him to another hospital. She seemed very close to him, smiling and he could feel the warmth from her. Was she now flirting with him?

It seemed like a long wait, then the nurse came back and offered Zed a cup of tea, saying that in ten minutes or so they would take Ben to the other place. Zed refused the tea though; he did not feel safe drinking it.

It seemed a lot longer than ten minutes; in fact this whole episode so far seemed like several days but when they got outside it was still dark. Zed asked the time. It was three o'clock in the morning. They had only left the pub about four hours ago!

Soon they arrived at the other hospital and Zed followed as they wheeled Ben into a ward.

An extremely tall doctor approached Zed; he was quite lanky with long blond hair flowing behind his white coat, a stethoscope on his chest and a pair of spectacles that were much too big for him.

"Hi man," said the doctor, "What's he on? It's a bum trip I think, but do you think he tried suicide?"

The doctor did not seem to realise that Zed was seeing everything multi-coloured and distorted, and his brain was operating at least ten times faster than normal. Zed was listening but analysing everything said on several levels.

Why was the doctor calling him "man"? Was he a real doctor? Did doctors really talk about bum trips?

Zed did not want to tell that guy anything other than he was sure Ben had not tried suicide, that they had gone out drinking and then he had seen Ben take something but he did not know what it was.

The doctor character seemed to shrink in size and started to grin like a crazy man. A few more questions, not answered by Zed, and the white-coat guy who had somehow cut off most of his blond hair told him to go home and come back later.

So Zed left the hospital. Once outside he mused that he did not know where he was. He spotted two nurses and asked the time; it was now 7 o'clock. Time had passed very quickly since three o'clock. He asked what hospital it was. "West Norwich," one of the nurses answered.

"I have to get home to Earlham Road," he said, "Do you know if there is a bus going there?"

"Yes," replied the nurse. "Which part of Earlham Road?

"Near the Black Horse pub, said Zed.

"You can get a number 11 to the Castle," she explained, "then change and get number 27."

"OK, thanks," he nodded "Number 11 then 27!" Zed had no problem getting home but he did in fact walk. It was just about 30 minutes walking and the sun was shining; he felt good although he felt bad about Ben and was worried in case his landlord found out, or even the police.

He kept noticing that the numbers 2, 7, 11, 22 and 27 were everywhere and felt as if the Universe was trying to send him some sort of coded message.

He returned to the apartment, number 7. Chris was still asleep. Zed went to his own room, lay on the mattress and soon fell asleep. He awoke a while later and looked at his clock. It was 7 minutes past 11!

Zed still felt high; it was as if he had not been to sleep at all; but he had a strange memory of meeting Timothy Leary, the so-called "acid guru" and Jimi Hendrix. Leary had explained something about how the Universe was made of numbers and Hendrix had told him that music was numbers too.

Zed devised a plan; he would have breakfast and go back to the hospital to see Ben; after that he would go to see Ben's girlfriend lover, Denny, the wife of the chemist that had made the PCP and try to find out more about it. He hoped that he could leave the hospital with Ben.

So, Zed went back to the hospital. Again he walked and again he kept noticing the numbers, 2, 7, 11, 17, 22, 27. He asked himself what was the significance.

Was it some sort of message? Was it a mathematical sequence? Was it some sort of reference to somewhere on a map, or maybe to a passage in a book such as The Bible? Of course, soon it became a game of simply spotting the numbers.

When he arrived at the hospital ward, he was greeted by a Matron who said that the doctor wanted to see him before he could see Ben, but that Ben was awake and recovering from his ordeal. She led Zed into a small side-room, where a doctor in his white-coat and stethoscope uniform sat behind a desk. Zed thought he was like some sort of witch doctor.

"Hi man," said the doctor, "sit down please. I'd like to ask you what your friend Ben took last night, because it was a bummer trip for him. It's better for him if we know what he took and why in case it was a suicide attempt."

"No, I'm pretty sure he didn't try to kill himself," said Zed, "He'd been drinking beer all night then I think he took a pill or something but I don't know what it was."

Zed did not like the questions. His mind was operating on multiple levels.

Soon the doctor said he wished he knew and then told Zed to go out and along the corridor to room 7, at the end, where he could see Ben.

"Number 7? At the end?"

Ben was laying on his back alone in the small room, naked on a bed with bars at each side to stop him from falling out. As Zed approached, Ben looked up, looking startled.

"You are real! Wow I thought you were just part of my dream."

Ben explained that he had woken up and they said he was in hospital but the bed had bars on so he thought it weird and he may have been crazy. He said he had thought that Zed and the whole university time had been a dream. Then he said that he had been with Jimi Hendrix and Timothy Leary and they had given him some numbers: 2, 7 and 11.

Ben said that he had been instructed in the secret of eternal life. Somebody had told him that food was the cause of death and if we stopped eating and survived on only cosmic energy, we could live forever..

Zed was blown away for a while that Ben was talking about the same numbers and Hendrix and Leary although he didn't know about cosmic energy and not eating. He had eaten that day already, anyway.

Ben explained that he had woken up naked and didn't know where his clothes were. He said he wanted to see Denny. Zed promised to go to visit Denny at her house and tell her where Ben was.

On the way out he asked the Matron to give Ben his

clothes. She said that Ben was refusing to eat or drink so they were not releasing him, for his own good. He went back to Ben and told him. Ben was adamant that he was not eating or drinking anything. Zed left and took a walk across the city, about an hour or so, and arrived at Denny's place, knocked on the door and was let in by Denny herself. She was a slight but shapely lady with short fair hair and a good smile. She had a warm personality and Zed got on with her well, despite not really approving of her relationship with both Ben and her chemist husband, as he was friends with both of them.

Zed explained what had happened and that Ben was OK but still in hospital, but when he told her which hospital she asked about the doctor. But Zed could only describe him, he did not know the doctor's name. Yet is did seem to be the same doctor, Denny said, as the one that had treated her husband. So she explained that she could not go to visit Ben. Zed would have to go back to the hospital to tell him. She made some tea and cheese sandwiches for Zed and then she rolled a couple of joints, which they shared.

Zed left and walked back to the hospital, He went straight into the ward and to the end of the corridor to room 7, quickly past any nurse, matron or doctors that could be lurking in wait. He walked into the room and saw a middle-aged lady sitting on a chair next to Ben who was sitting up in bed, now dressed.

He introduced himself as Ben's friend and the lady said she was Ben's mother, from London. The hospital had called her. She asked Zed what he had given Ben. She was blaming Zed!

So it had become complicated now.

Ben's mother was blaming Zed.

The doctor said Ben could go after he had eaten and drank something.

Ben did not want to.

Ben's mother would only take him if he went back to London with her.

Ben would only go to London if Zed went along.

Denny and Ben would not be seeing each other for a while.

Chris was back at the apartment probably wondering what was happening; Ben and Zed would have to go there to pack some clothes.

Zed knew he was still under the effect of the PCP and he knew Ben was probably still tripping. He realised that it was going to be upon him to persuade Ben to eat and drink and get him out of there.

It surprised him when a few logical words to Ben later, having told him straight and simply that if he did not eat they were not going to let him go, Ben agreed to eat bread and some fruit and to drink water.

And so it was that the pair of them went to London and stayed a few days at Ben's parent's flat, way up in a high-rise block near Swiss Cottage.

The two lads agreed that they had both actually had a good time and the following day they felt normal.

Ben had arranged to have his eyes tested the next day.

They both went out, smoked a couple of joints and Ben went to the opticians.

He later told Zed that the eye test was stupid and it was just lights moving around.

When Ben got the spectacles, he tried them once and then he threw them away.

Believe in Nothing!
Just Don't Believe in Anything Else.

LIFE OF JOY

Drifting I am, through time and space,
Not mine but at some other pace,
Knowing ahead what I'll inevitably face,
What keeps me here is simple Grace.

Above and below an endless cloud,
Naked whilst wrapped in a Human shroud,
Have felt ashamed and also felt so proud,
Sometime alone or one in a crowd.

The light is shining, the music plays,
The joy of peace within is played,
Beyond the senses that surely fade,
Outside the thoughts that made me afraid,

I've been happy and also sad,
Seen some good and seen some bad,
But on the whole, I'd say I'm glad,
And grateful for the life that I have had.

"Value the spaces."

IN HIS HAT
by Ivor S Garfield (RIP)

I've seen something inside my hat.
Dreams and visions, assure you of that.
The chap that wears me knows an awful lot,
He's artistic and clever and fits that slot.

Me and my pal together smoked some
Of the best hashish, some awesome. We travelled the
70's, you bet your stash, To go to great places, find
the best hash.

Across to India, we sampled delights.
Those beautiful people, shame for their plights,
Yet there we found more hashish to smoke,
Met great people and shared a toke.

It's a most pleasurable hat,
Comfy and cosy through smoking all that,
And when he sleeps, I feel secure,
My buddy who wears me makes me sure.

Yes, I can honestly say it's been a pleasure,
To have been a part of all this leisure.
I was meant to sit on my buddy's head.
But I always wondered why his eyes were red.

God bless him now, wherever he is,
I miss him so; he was 'The Biz'
A connoisseur - that's definitely right,
The people still say that Hat's out-of-sight.

OTHER HEADS

Drawn by Rocky van de Benderskum

IN LOVING MEMORY OF

Chris Baldwin
Dottie Baldwin
Dave "Woofer" Barker
Don Barnard
Jackie Barnard
Eagle Bill
Elizabeth Brice (Clare Hodges)
John Cripps
Colin Campbell Clarke Michael Cutler
Patrick 'Patman' Denning
Eddie Ellison
Michael Fell
Paul Flynn (MP)
Paul Fowler
Ivor Garfield
Jack Herer
Tom Hanson
Elizabeth 'Biz' Ivol
Derek Large
Chris Lausch
Maggie May
Levi McCarthy
Dr John Morgan
Colin Paisley
Mark Palmer
"Uncle" Michael Pryce
Nol van Shaik
Phil Stovell
Bill Reeve
'Grannie' Pat Tabram
Stuart Talbot
Dr Lynn Zimmer

SOME SKETCHES

by

JACQUI MALKIN

Jacqui discovered she could draw when awarded art prize at school. She attended Blackpool college of technology and art (pre diploma),Norwich school of art (graphic design) and worked in a design studio as junior general artist. Jacqui painted on cars and coaches, leather goods for fairs, tattoo designs and sold, bartered and gave away her stuff! Jacqui volunteered as art tutor. She did a degree in multimedia that she says was a waste of time, as computer technology changed too fast but learnt Photoshop. She was inspired by American comics, Beardsley, pre-Raphaelites amongst others.

FE and QT in “The Effie Enigma”

ZX in "The Effie Enigma"

Effie Fifty in
"The Effie Enigma"

QT in
"The Effie Enigma"

SOME POEMS

by

MELISSA DOORDAUGHTER

On the frozen seas of Northern Europe, Melissa heard poetry calling. Kullervo and Ilmarinen accompanied her in Ibiza. Whilst many were dancing in discos, she was weaving magic and the future, leaving messages in bottles and singing on the beach. She can be found in Red Tents, Dutch squats, cob buildings and apple orchards, looking for the muse. At present, she has published "For precise reason (by A. Snail)" and "Fragments of Her Story", two collections of poetry and prose. The authors she most admires are Aldous Huxley, Mervyn Peake and Agatha Christie.

http://www.buffry.org.uk/fragmentsofherstory.html

MARY JANE SPEAKS

Some call me marijuana- to you it's Mary Jane
But just like Shakespeare's roses, my buds still smell the same.
When Shiva fetched me down from the mountains
And called me 'the holiest of plants'
He knew that I would help him
In the Most Auspicious Dance.

You can look from any angle
But still my friend will see
That I am indeed friend to all-
All who would be free.

Free from hunger I can keep you
With my most nutritious seed
And I can stop the deserts encroaching
If it's a rich top-soil you need.

You can be free to keep the forests
(Don't sacrifice the trees to false idol Office Gods)
For I can give you plenty o'fibre
If it's paper that you want.

I can help you with your sickness-
Open that third and inner eye-
Help you find your appetite,
If you will only try.

For those sick with AIDS or anorexia or chemotherapy
I can give you a case of the munchies
If you have a taste of me.

If you've got spasms that you can't control
Or your eyes with glaucoma feel uptight
Just take a dose of Ole Red Eye
And you will feel alright.

If it's PMT that ails you
Or you're faced with labour pains
Let Mother Mary relieve you
And open up the way.

Antispasmodic, Exotopic
And if that's not enough
I can make fuel, food, cloth, rope, oil, soap
And lots of other stuff.

But a little word in your ear,
You're third ear if you please,
If you are already hearing voices
Then it is not me you need.

I'm no great use to schizophrenics,
With too much dopamine in their brains,
And if you're blood pressure is too low, beware,
I am Great Medicine but still you must take care.

THE RED SHOES REVISITED

Once upon a time there was a girl called Karen. Karen's family were very poor. She was so poor that she didn't even have a father. Her mother was sick: sometimes Karen would find her on the floor in the kitchen, unable to stand up. Sometimes her mother would drink wine and sleep all afternoon. While her mummy was sleeping Karen would go outside and play with old plastic bottles, filling them up with daisies and water, and pretend she had made a magic potion that would cure her disease. Or she may stay indoors and watch television.

On the television she saw pictures of beautiful princesses and queens dripping with diamonds. Then she would look down at her own faded T-shirt, that was given to her in a black bin-bag by the woman who owned the sweetshop at the bottom of the road. She wished that she could have a wonderful dress with a sparkling train and a pearl-embroidered bodice.

Meanwhile, Karen's mother was getting sicker. Her hair all fell out so she had to cover her head with a scarf, and she began to lean on a walking stick when she left the house.

One day she called Karen into the living-room. In front of her was a small wooden box with a swan engraved on the lid.

"Karen, Darling," her mother said, "I have got a present for you."

Out of the box she gently lifted a beautiful necklace. It had a silver chain and a large pendant, round and smooth like a stone that has lay on the bed of a river for a long time. The stone sparkled in the sun and Karen saw that it was a beautiful emerald green - the same colour as her mother's eyes.

As Karen's mother fastened it around her daughter's throat she said "This belonged to my mother, and her mother before that. I want you to have it now and remember that while you wear it, your mother's love, and the love of all the women in your family, is with you."

Soon after that Karen's mother died. Karen too thought she would die of sadness. But when she went out into the garden to cry, the little daisies lifted up their heads and said "Behold the glorious sun!". And so she went into her bedroom to cry alone under the blankets, where the daisies could not disturb her, but when her tears fell on the green gem around her neck, it began to glow and a warmth washed through her heart, and she felt that her mother wasn't so far away after all.

Karen was sent to live with a distant relative who she had never seen before. He was a tall man with a big round belly like a pregnant woman, and he was very rich. His house was always shining and clean, full of heavy wooden furniture and an enormous marble fireplace with a great roaring fire. But when Karen went to play in the garden, there were no daisies there, only cement and gravel and any little weed that did grow was pulled up straight away. He gave her a little room with a lock on the door and let her do whatever she wanted as long as she arrived home at dinner time with clean hands and a clean face and a pretty dress on.

One day the man told her that she must scratch his head for him for 5 minutes, and then he would buy her a box of chocolates.

He sat on the floor in front of her and she scratched his head through his greasy thick hair. And the next day he came home with a big box of chocolates, tied up with a golden ribbon, the most delicious chocolates she had ever tasted: strawberry creams, bitter dark chocolate, and even one in the shape of a heart. She took them out into the garden and ate them all up in one go. That night she felt sick, but she kept the golden ribbon to put in her hair.

The following evening the man said if she rubbed his neck for 10 minutes, he would buy her a pair of new shoes. So she rubbed his fat neck, pretending she was kneading soft dough to make bread, and sure enough the next day he gave her a pair of new shoes. She opened the box and found them nestled in among pink crepe paper, a pair of gleaming ruby red shoes, complete with sparkling stones on the buckles: and fit for a queen. Karen wore her new shoes everywhere, even though they were tight across her toes and rubbed her heels raw. Everybody said what a lucky girl Karen was, to be cared for so well, and Karen would nod her head and try to look grateful; but the green stone that lay across her heart was silent and felt cold against her breast.

One morning, not long after Karen had received her red shoes, she woke up to find a heavy weight upon her. It was her adopted father: he was laying on top of her, pushing his thick tongue into her mouth. She was disgusted and so surprised that she froze in fright, she kept her eyes shut tight, hoping that if she pretended to be asleep, he would go away. Eventually he did. When he got up and shut the door she resolved to keep her bedroom locked from then on.

But when she locked the door the man would complain, saying how sad he was to be left all alone and how ungrateful Karen was to shut him out after everything he had done for her. Then Karen felt sadder and more alone than ever but the amulet round her neck glowed a soothing green and she heard the wind in the trees whisper "Fear not, Karen, for we are with you."

The next day when she got up, Karen found no weight upon her, and when she went to prepare breakfast, she found him cold, stone dead in his chair, his eyes wide open and his tongue lolling, purple, out of his mouth.

Karen thought she ought to feel sad but her heart soared and she could hear birds singing in the garden.

She quickly threw on an old dress and had her hand on the doorknob when she saw her red shoes. They were sitting neatly by the door, the red gems winking at her in the light, as if to say "Are we not fair and lovely?" So Karen squeezed them on and ran out into the half light of the early morning. There was a rain falling but Karen cared not. She lifted her arms up to the sky and gave a whoop of joy. It didn't seem enough to express her feelings of relief, to be free of the old man and his heavy, heavy house. So she called out again "I'm so glad that he is dead, I will dance on his fat head" and this time she wiggled her hips and she waved her arms and she stretched her fingers, kicked her legs and turned a pirouette. And as she spun, her blood suddenly turned cold at the thought that maybe someone would see her and they would know what a bad girl she was for celebrating the death of her benefactor.

Karen tried to stop, to look and see if she had been seen, but her feet continued now of their own accord to move in some jolly dance steps.

She danced out of the garden and into the street, thinking that she could go down to the beach where no-one would see her but when she tried to go left, her feet carried her right, and when she tried to slow down, her shoes carried her along faster and faster, until she reached the end of the road, and was going over the wrought iron bridge that led to the park.

Karen felt frightened now and she lifted up her legs, trying to pull the red shoes off her feet, but they were stuck tight and carried her on, through the town and into the surrounding countryside.

She was still dancing when night fell, her clothes torn by ten thousand brambles, her skin scratched, her limbs weary and her face slack and empty, exhausted.

The night was worse than the day, a cold, pregnant moon looked down on Karen and the Man in the Moon's mouth formed an 'o' of surprise, as if to say what a cruel girl Karen was to dance so. Karen was scared as she danced through the lonely cemetery and as the owls hooted and the bats flitted through the sky, Karen was frightened that the spirits of the dead would come and berate her for being a cold, heartless child.

When morning came Karen was still dancing. She came to a river, with a house beside it, hidden by the reeds. There, next to the house was a dwarf. He was chopping wood. His long beard was red like a fox's pelt and his eyes glinted as sharp as his axe. He stopped for a moment as Karen danced by.

"That's a fine pair of dancing shoes you've got there," he said.

"Please! Please! I'd do anything to be rid of them!" Karen cried out. "I'd do anything- please chop them off so I can rest!"

The man stroked his beard. "Anything, huh? Well I could do with a young lady to help around the place. The missus isn't as young as she once was, you know…" He picked up his axe. "Come closer child," he said in a voice that was almost a whisper.

As he lifted his axe to strike a shrill voice came from the house calling "John? John? Who's that out there?"

A door opened next to the wood pile and an old lady emerged, all round and red faced, with a scarf over her head.

"This young lady has asked me to cut her feet off," replied John, now looking more like a sheep than a fox.

"Oh she has, has she? And what would a pretty dancing girl be wanting that for, here at the river's edge, with only the cows and reeds for company?"

"Please!" cried Karen once more. "I can't stop- the shoes won't let me rest!"

The woman strode over to Karen and took hold of her shoulders with two strong, capable hands, and as Karen's feet kicked and jerked to an invisible tune, the woman embraced Karen, engulfing her with the smells of soured milk and fresh bread. She whispered hot in Karen's ear "Get away, girl, no good will come of you here," and then she released Karen from her grip and looked her straight in the eyes without flinching, her eyes as grey as slate, as cold as the Northern seas.

"You will stop dancing when you see that the dance never ends" she pronounced. "Now go! We've got work to do. No time have we for ballerinas,". She gave a sharp nod to her husband, who turned to continue chopping wood.

Poor Karen, what could she do? Away she went, along the river bank, past cows and windmills. Day and night she danced.

One day she heard above her the familiar cry of the seagull and felt the tang of salt in the air. She had reached the ocean and longed to wash her feet in the waves. Upon the beach she danced, her shoes becoming heavy with sand, the sound of the water hitting the shore soothing, like a lullaby that is only half remembered. Try as she might, Karen tried to dance in to the waters, but the more she tried, the more the shoes became agitated and blocked her way. Karen felt that if she could not free herself from the curse, then she may as well drown herself and join her mother in her grave.

Karen tried to go to the water but she found herself spinning, round and round, until everything around her became a blur of colour. She felt hot and dizzy, as if she was about to be sick. At that moment she became aware of the gem hanging at her breast, and a voice whisper " Look! Look to yourself Karen!"

Karen looked down at herself, her tattered dress, her arms splayed out as she tried to keep her balance and she looked at her white hands, her fingers reaching out, out towards nothing.

"Oh forgive me mother" she whispered in a silent prayer.

"Oh innocent Karen, there is nothing to forgive" came the words from her green stone, and through her tears Karen looked at her little hand and realised, as she spun out of control upon the beach, that her hand was the only thing she could see clearly, the only thing that seemed not to move. As she watched it, her dizziness faded. She gave a deep sigh of relief, realising that she herself was that still point of the ever spinning wheel, and as she sighed the stone upon her chest rose and fell like a boat upon the ocean, and she laughed with surprise to realise that throughout her dancing, throughout everything, the invisible dance of the breath had been with her, silent and untiring.

As she laughed the spell broke as suddenly as a mirror shatters into a thousand pieces and she fell down into the cold grey water that covered her like a blanket, soaking her to the bone, washing away the grime of guilt and stains of tears, soothing her flushed cheeks, cool and refreshing as her mother's kiss. Finally the ocean washed those red shoes off her feet and they drifted out towards the horizon, bobbing up and down to the never-ending melody of the ocean.

From that day, Karen was free.

LOWESTOFT

There's no excuse for going to Lowestoft,
It's at the end of the line.
But if you will tell me your reason for going,
Then I will tell you mine. (surplus space)
My mother lived there long ago
And then one day she died
I gave her ashes to the Northern Sea
And cried and cried and cried.
Now I know I must return there
To the Gates of Hell
To walk through the cement and cemeteries
And smell the "Birds Eye" smell.
Oh this tiny town, grown to such a twisted shape
Where all the men are monkeys
And the best of them an Ape.
They know the danger in the air
The peril of walking streets at night
Of vicious be-clawed children
Who love to maim and fight
Of the strange artists that live underground
In single, darkened rooms
Waiting to relieve their karma
And singing haunting tunes.
Beware the friendly stranger
Who, smiling, will take your hand
And introduce you to the paedophile
That drives the ice-cream van.
Ah, but there is a tender beauty
In that bruised and silent place
The beauty of the abandoned,
The long forgotten space.

And like the concrete wall
That barricades the houses against the sea.
I try to deny the piece of this town
That resides inside of me.
Oh but to see that ocean dawn,
The town of the absolute East
Where the angels come to play
Hide and seek with Beast.

SEVEN BEDROOM HOUSE

Reality does not fit into rooms without mirrors
The moon, half full, keeps some secrets.
There is no way into the room without a mirror
There is no redemption for the hardened sinner
You know what I'm saying –keep the curtains drawn-
No one will see you then.
Reality does not fit into rooms without mirrors
Small is the difference a reflection makes
Even with the door shut the light does not move
Even in the low light it isn't really you.
I dreamt last night of leaving the seven bedroom house
And the room without a mirror
I saved my skin for a reason
Though I could pay the ransom
Of the man who owned the mirror.
Warning, my lady- I am not confused and I dream
I left the seven bedroom house.
Reality does not fit into the room without a mirror
I dreamt last night I dreamt that you had never been a sinner
Love never been a sin
I'd like to see my face again
Show me where to begin.

Not in the first bedroom where the curtains are bright pink,
And not in the second where there is a mouldy sink,
(sink or stink? Bedroom?)
No, not the third, with the mirrors polished bright
And not in the fourth where I know you sleep at night

The fifth I feel is a tad too small
The sixth a tad too big

Let it be the seventh room, the room
Where the secrets live.

Reality does not fit into rooms without mirrors
And the moon, half full, keeps some secrets.
Notes pass under doors
Notes flawed travel on the breeze
I tried to wash myself clean of all the secrets
And surreptitious burnings
I held my head stiff and high
But did not have the keys for the room without a
mirror.
Last night you must have heard me calling you
I saved my skin for a reason
Though I could pay the ransom
I saw into the heart of the man who owned the mirror
And I know you heard me scream.

If only you'd warned me
Heart beat
You heard me calling
Next week
If only you'd asked me
Guess-work was never your friend
Heart beat lemon scent wanted defeat
Heart beat
            Heart beat
                        Heart beat
You take after your father
                        Heart beat
I'm after your soul

Heart beat
You look like a martyr
But you know I'm not fooled.

It's not clear what happened in history
If it was even a mirror at all
And what's behind your face is a mystery
Though I bet your stories are tall

Did I jump? I won't say much
Just know I hit the ground
And we will fly one day dear
Like we're used to holding hands.

Classic cut angel worth two on the pin
The warmth of another is the worth of
My thin melting ice gift
So damn cold it burns
My thin melting ice gift
Protects a heart that yearns

The moon will be full next Saturday
More secrets to reveal
The moon will be full and fatter then
Maybe our dreams will be sealed
Vibrating shaking morrow
Whole and empty hand
Touch me starlight touch me
And your wish is my command.

I'LL GIVE YOU THE FREUDIAN SLIP

As he climbed the stone staircase
Icarus counted the steps,
Just as his father did before him.

I had never known my father
I was jealous of Icarus for that reason.

In a way I am jealous of all men.
I covet their power.

I wanted to take Icarus to the room
At the top of the stairs and dress him
In woman's clothing
Groom his golden locks and fleece
Anoint his feet
Kiss his feet
Steal his manhood
Then steal the wings, and be away
Out the window.

Icarus let me, with
A statues masked smile
Unlock the door.

Snow fell on the beaches.
Thistles grew there too.

The greed for power took control of my soul
I had stolen his wings
But only he and I knew
Only he and I knew
That I was stolen too.

THE PSYCHOLOGY OF THE GIFT

Built a power station with my frustration

Rung the scene of devastation with a haze of hesitation

I muffled my screams with a broken drum

I beat the beat but did I wait too long?

As inside I churned and yelled I gave a gulp 'cos I never felt

This large before too large to hold

Insatiable angel you broke the mould.

I'm lighter than feathers and brighter than light

Guess I look lower than low when I'm soaring the heights

And I'll try not to scream as you kiss me goodnight

Because frustration builds a furnace like a rupture beneath the skin

And although my love flows in earnest I can not will not give in

It was never a choice not to absolve the sin

And it's the same as incest because we're keeping it all in

School girl slave girl wishing well thief

School girl you smell you give me the creeps

Vanity is vanquished because there's no room at the edge

You must maintain frustration when you are living on a ledge

Now you've sold away your body and you've lost sight of your soul

You turn around to find yourself and all you finds a hole

You've given away everything and you find them asking "more"

And you would have slept away the years if you hadn't been so sore

But you must maintain frustration because that's the only thing you have left

And I know you stayed frustrated because I was watching from the bit that's not "to let"

Maintaining your frustration was what set you apart

And living so frustrated is such a fucking art

It's walking on a tightrope when the ends are out of sight

It's remembering that you can see when there's never any light

And I never could surrender even when the moods they drove me down

I was always frozen solid from the neck right down

And I hunger for a thawing now

To let my slave girl dance

But I choose to be frustrated then so I know that there's a chance

That I must remain a captive here inside this chilly shed

Emotional hypothermia seems inevitable if on snow you've fed

But I feel so hot so hot so hot so hot from inside out

I feel like I'm a burning cage I need to be let out

Of my frustration- the psychology of the gift-

I'd rather have me nothing than to drown

In this snow drift.

GRANDMA

When they raped me I tried to keep calm
Lest my soul should come to deep harm
Then they tortured my mother and tore out her eyes
Lest she should see through her masters disguise
And grandmother, you stood, silent and strong
A tree unshaken by all that went on
Always you knew that the passing of time
Would leave forgotten the most heinous of crimes
Now the flowers still blossom and the rivers still flow
And all the mountains are still capped with snow
But beneath your silent foliage, are you asleep?
As the rivers still flow still the women weep
Behind aprons and kitchens, and hatred of whores
Behind masks of make-up are souls that still soar
And some men they make slaves of their women,
their wife
And then they wonder why they feel imprisoned for
life

But grandmother, she is not asleep
And as we sow, so shall we reap
They suffocate her with cement, try to poison her
womb
Choke the blue skies with their man-made perfume
Yet nothing is as strong as the soul that seeks the truth
And grandmother lives on, in beauty and youth.

SOLID SEEMS OUR BOND

As tough as it is strong

But now I see what rests on me

And has done all along.

Of all the times I've watched your face

Lips poised, neck arched with grace.

Still silence warms my heart

And I understand that we should be together

Forever

Never to part.

Solid seems our bond,

As tough as it is strong

But before I didn't know the truth

That love will sacrifice my youth

Leave me loved, secure,

Stranded and bored

Each face on the street a new lesson ignored

Another path I have not travelled

While we, shackled happily,

Ignore these lives, lessons and lusts

And follow the yellow brick road

To stagnancy.

THE ASTRAL SUPERMARKET

I woke at the astral supermarket
Where a lone tree grows
And as I wandered through the aisles
And the astral tins of beans
I found a single bluebell
Now I wonder what it means

Change is the essence of time
The time has changed

I was searching for your house
On the day you disappeared
I was looking for you for a reason
Though I wasn't sure quite why
And I must have walked past your house
At least fifteen times
But when I passed it
I didn't see it
I was blind blind blind

And like the scars upon your cheeks
And the bruises on your body
Some words, you know, are empty
Some apologies not sorry.
And I would search the seven kingdoms
For a picture of your love
Volunteer my hollow patience
Petition all the stars
Beg the solid earth, my dear,
To find your missing heart

The extent of my debts
I only now am learning
All the times with you I was spending
When I thought that I was earning.
What is my love, pray tell,
But dust thrown against the sun?
What does it mean,
This throne to fill,
If it must be done alone?

You'd hidden your house for a reason
And I was certain the reason was me
You'd hidden yourself for a reason
To state the matter simply.
We couldn't see
We couldn't see
We were blind and bound to be
Tattoos upon the enemy
Because we couldn't see.

THE BALLAD OF THE BARDO

O the becoming

I include the wavering,
The moving growing waiting changing
And here we see the spectrum splitting
Join again before rebounding.

O the becoming
The arrival and the going
The thirst the quenching and the reason.
It becomes a toddlers kisses freely given,
A purple sky becoming vision,
It becomes a rain I long to be in,
A hard earned rest from long felt feeling.
Waking up in slow motion,
Freedom, or submission, to compulsion.
It becomes you in the lover's kiss
And in the people I love to miss

O becoming the bodies sigh,
The flickering lids in the dreamer's eye
The tears that hurt, the taste of pain,
The heavy sob and hoarse ripped scream,
Shocked and empty, feeling full
Leaking bubbles and dentist drills
The sheen upon the pool of oil
And in the biscuit and in the weevil,

It becomes you now to fear your fate
becomes you now to hate the wait
becomes a time when all has changed
becomes a rhyme becoming lame

but O the becoming

Sitting back upon the journey
Feeling a love for the fear of the mystery
Of the hard struggle to break through the shell
Of all the crimes and all the hell
That burns on out or smoulders gently
And in half an hour I'm feeling angry
And then it goes
So feeling silly
And now and now
o look at me
I'm becoming
becoming
          going

See?

HYMN FOR THE GODDESS

Can you see me?
I am Persephone
Underground for cycles three
Red red seed then
Liberty.

Persephone has now grown older
The corn mother
Fair Demeter
Bless the land
And bless the harvest
Rejoice for the triple Goddess
Sitting at the spinning wheel
Time to think- to do- to feel

And so the seasons change
Once more
A cross roads
An open door
'Twixt holy virgin
And sacred whore
All Hail Hecate
Keeper of the lore.

The Triple Goddess
Dwells in the shadow
Under the earth
In the meadow
Every bird her praises sing
Sky lark- black birds- red robin

Every woman made in her image
Blessed of breast and pleasing visage
Charmer of snakes
Keeper of the grain
A sacred chalice, a secret name.

Blessed be the ever changing form
Mother dusk and her daughter Dawn
Let it be
That we will see
She is us and we are she.

SOME POEMS

by

ARIADNE SNAIL

http://www.buffry.org.uk/fragmentsofherstory.html

Melissa is a graduate in Anthropology and Religion at the University of Lampeter, Wales and works as a teacher. She has published "For precise reason (by A. Snail)" and "Fragments of Her Story", two collections of poetry and prose.
The authors she most admires are Aldous Huxley, Mervyn Peake and Agatha Christie.
"Surely it's obvious,
Doesn't every school-boy know it?
Ends are ape chosen, only the means are man's."
From Ape and Essence (Aldous Huxley)

THE WEDDING GUESTS

The oldest woman here wears a crown

Of hawthorn berries and vines twisted round

The knots in her hands like the roots of trees

Help her to count all her laughters and griefs.

The gap in her teeth and the light in her eyes

Show me her way is authentic and wise.

And together we brush and comb the grey hair

Of her companion, the Green Man,
who waits for her where

By the light of the moon and the call of the Owl

He stands watch throughout triumph and trial.

IF WE CAN GET THROUGH "THE CRISIS" WITHOUT A WORLD WAR, WE WILL HAVE MADE A MAJOR STEP IN OUR EVOLUTION.

The body is dead but the light in her eyes
Is energy that can't be destroyed,
And his grandma has already seen so oft
The rises and falls of economic flux

That neither holds wonder or fear for her now
Whose seen so often the seasons go round.
And the spots in the sun have a cycle of twenty-four years
Which then effects global economy

Through the harvest of golden wheaten ears.
And how many of my fore-mothers
Made daisy chains in the grass
While world politics were changed
And fashions went rolling past?

EXILED FROM THE LAND OF THE DEAD

The dead leave no instructions
- and how could they?
Where is the room for echoes in a hijacked world,
Where meaning is sold and sold and thrice sold,
Where life, we're told, is dreams on webs of markets and production,
Where meaning spins around the adverts, the customs are pre-packaged,
Altering with the markets mores?
And my understanding of the spirit is something purchased:
A word detached from any feeling
but the purse's ache
And the keen dreaming of a folk fed on solid identity.

The dead leave no instructions in the cemetery.
I have checked.
No instruction but cold reminders: tomb stones like failing flowers
They stop in silence, never reaching any goal but one.
I looked, in hope, to escape the shop and stream
Or find some deeper meaning in compulsive buying
But the dead leave no instruction, like dead leaves in the autumn.

Fallen and trodden, the random colours will distract me for a time
From the towers and the pits of my own mind
Yet may return me there again.

The dead need no instruction,
and why should they?
Buying and selling are easy in a land where life is currency
And falling and weeping are equally smooth,
Giving words you can trust to feelings you can't lose:
They will prove the law, the writ and facts,
Give good solid reasons why you can't relax
But I ask you to lean back into premature rigor mortis
And the death of the herd,
And to see where the exile begins, and from there
Walk forward.

Febbraio, o meglio, la mese della febbre.

Dripping month
Wreathed mountains waiting invisible
Under the blanket of fog and damp.
Four days of faces flushes
Red and sweaty
The only colour left
In a world of greys and browns.
Rotten month,
Waiting month,
Puzzles and old stories
Told again again.
Coughing month, and cabbage,
Garlic and onion month
Medicine and protestations.

Poem for Saint Valentine

Feb 14th 2016

Sometimes love is not enough to hold two souls together.
I loved the lake, twin soul with the sky.
But what can one do
About a promise made to a dead man?
Because I promised I wouldn't swim
In those lakes again
After 6 stitches
And another cut three months later.
I promised not to go
Naked as a seal
Nor slip between those silver silken sheets
To lose myself in sky and water.
And isn't that the goal of love?
To lose ones self in the other?
And isn't that the first fear too?
That the self should slip away,
Vanish like a pebble in the lake
Sink in silence, gone forever?
The sky was on fire, an open wound
The night they took me to the sacred lake.
We stood on the shore. I had been there before.
But this time, not to swim.

Tetrahydrocannabinol

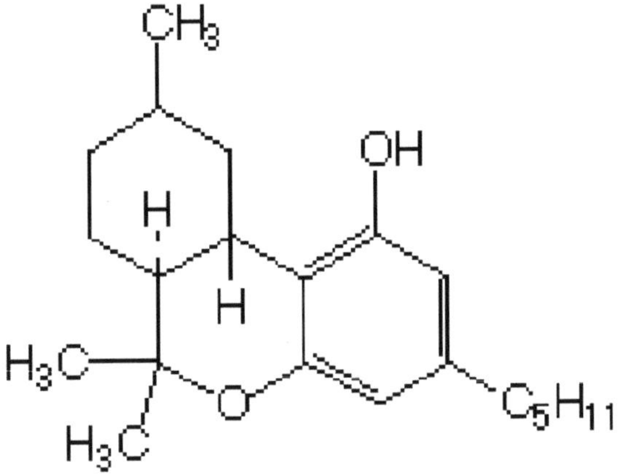

CH_3

OH

H

H

H_3C

O

C_5H_{11}

H_3C

SOME POEMS

by

STEVE COOK

Steve Cook is the son of a Norfolk farming family, an artist, poet, traveller and mechanic. He is the author of a series of "Natural Allies" poetry compilations. A graduate of Norwich Arts School

HMP CADIZ

Life is the high mountain in the stream
That comes like a river and into my dream.
Looks like I can't see it now.
Seems like I can't hear
Cities drawing near.

Long in one mountain, high in the scream,
That comes like a river and into my dream.
Colours turning read
In the eyes of my head
As I wake and rise from my bed

CRUNCH

©Steve Cook 2015

At the rise of the twisting of facts
Like an inhuman wish to falsify acts,
Within its means, a bunch of twisting dreams
And uncertain lies. The Crunch. Their pious schemes
Falsify award with self-seeking
Using educational good will and notoriety.
Humanity! Like detritus feeding fish,
And children, simply believing a wish.

Material harmony, struggling to protect,
Like a language with a simple dialect
Passion, like a moist wind coming with a beautiful scent
Of heather aroma, calms the mind.
So now we must invent
A way through of these complexities.

And you? With a new ego inflamed
Accelerating towards change
Rocking our brains.
New standards to our names,
Everybody complains.
It is lessening the bounty within our store
And we're put off by an impossible score.
I wish it were as before,
For us to rearrange later.
It's a hard climb to remain the same
And sometimes we are truly 'up against it',
Yet you have new images for us to fit.

A SHAFT OF LIGHT IN A DUSTY PLACE

©Steve Cook 2015

The sun within the atomic element,
Through a glass pane it shines.
As if through a diamond it gleams:
Instilling warmth in the dusty atmospheric space–
A comfort on our faces while we absorb
Vitamin 'D'.
Into the water the sun does both,
Warming and glistening
Like a sparkling stream.
Gravity plays an integral part:
When the warm air rises
And frost its power prizes.
Opening rooted rocks from high pinnacles.

Time passes, we've One planet
To arrest the sun in positive ways;
This is a fact, it's how we react
Together we're open to its cause.
We must develop proper uses of its power
After all, we are touched by its light.
Everyone hopes children will grow up bright,
Individual too, with the roots of common sense.
When we wake up, all thoughts rush:
Birds chirping in the moist bush
Eating red berries and the like—
I'm off and away, composing on my bike!

RED SQUIRRELS

Listen here, if I were pulling the string
I'd change almost everything.
Rid the forests of the American Grey
Like the coypu it's been terror long enough
Yes, that'll be an end to that.

I'd like to see an end to horror and disease
See creatures happy and at ease
March hares o'er fields of muddy maize
The moonlight's clear, escaping clouds sparked their craze.
Not so depressing, admiring willows bending in the breeze

.
The native fox used to compliment
Red squirrel dealing with its nuts
Hurrying about like royalty with condiment.
Then there's the magpie whose character is doubtful
He goes robbing nests, about in the wood

And he calls as if to make his strategy clear
They're used to the human element, precocious in fear
And his peculiarity, He knows he'll never fit
But in hops of beauty, he absolves his despair.
So don't try to tell us 'it's all the same'

It's harder to keep your pecker up! It's a bleaker game
It's rougher when you walk alone, down a country lane.
That in nature's melding, all these creatures politely
syncopate
Lazily they pass summer days, til collecting begins afore
the wintry slumber.

The mind breathes with the organically nutritious food to
share
They all go about as if they still lived in a medieval age
They're much more resourceful: they learn each bit well
And only wish for peace here, and if you want to know
Only at dawn does the Raven freely roam.

A cocky little bird strutting, swaggering as if to say
He's the real magician, who'll sit upon a headstone of
sombre grey. sombre grey.

THE UNIVERSALITY OF TRUST

The cupboards of my mind are empty
I'm searching at a loss to find,
The energy itself to struggle along:
I might have used repetition too much
Fall from grace; be out of touch.

Black as the feelings;
Shady become the dealings
But from the frame-work; the competence
The logic, mind building brick;
Even when, I'm right at the end of my wick
I'll try and make the right times stick.

The cupboards of my mind; are full
So full are they I travel lightly blind
I'll try and speak from sense
I know not, where it came from whence
Waken up, and not be so dense:
The reasoning is part of the spirit
All the confrontation one can save,
I'll try and be more brave
Not give into the instance, I am on a wave!

I'll try and tally unto
And be generally true
For an everlasting vibe came through
Out there on the edge of space
The stars shone too;
And covered the Earth in dust
To filter the light that came through
In the universality of trust.

THE SEASON TO BE

I'm searching to be true,
Away from emptiness and depth.
Just struggling through:
Trying to find a key to turn to let me through
'Cause there's very little else for me to do.
Too materialistic, weighing me down:
Eating disorder,
Ambitious dreams, fractious beginnings;
Never grasping the energy all-abounding
Of the friends, these whims surrounding.
Time to flow, brief release from duty,
Welding in relief the beauty,
Trusting where the bonds seem supple;
Sights on a winning double
A rainbow arc for all the trouble.

Participation for the duration:
But no-one wants it at their door:
Unloading burdens, expectedly like trees in autumn,
Thinning out the posing complexity,
Like painting with dexterity.
No knowing the whys and wherefores,
An abstract knowledge,
Within I'm searching to be true,
Up from the depths of emptiness.
A life to fulfil, an omnipresent will,
Defend one's ways
Allegorical as the days.

The world is full of trickery
In search of the distance.
A little time to think sensibly
And breathe the breath of happiness.
To keep one's treasures nearby
However humble this humility;
Trying not to be discordant with virtue,
Or lost in the rigours of simplicity:
Regain once more the social cue
And wit enough to think for others.
The laughter she shines the view flowing slow 'n' easy
Of these surrenders I knew.
When I was light in the mind just now made easy.

SAD ENVIRONMENTALIST

I feel a little disenchanted
Like the protectors at the Gates of Hell;
A notion of stupidity and an idea of what's going on
No strength in the muscles,
Too bewildered to break into what might have been,
Too docile to jump from the fire,
Lethargically wrapped in futility;
Resigned, or designed, to drop
From God's equanimity,
The bottom room in the house of life.
How many times can we awake,
As we begin to slip passively
Further into the abyss?
How many chances must we waste
Before we join in the journey through the stars,
Between each galaxy, lifting up
Through the in-between and to sleep like brothers
In the knowledge of what we ought to have done,
Not what we ended up doing or might have been?
Then you think: If they think this about me and I am.

In the effect the same as a child (the soul of which
Includes those starving in backward social situations)
My father must be sad also; and you slip into a
Psychosis of anguish your life, your intimate friend
Cease to inspire one's destiny.
You are ostracised from knowledge of yourself,
As those streaming past the Gates of Hell. Simply
Think... Simply think... You will not realise

You're devastated to the extent that your body is giving Up the Ghost:

Your mind sad with cares loaded against

Your understanding, and you have to adjust on such occasions

We are brought up to be peaceful

As a child of the Universe:

We tend to think of the Earth

With gut reaction:

Akin to that, we return to our mother (Mother Earth)

The milk of life on which we are weaned,

Adapting to our circumstance.

Do unto others as you would them unto you.

Continue along different openings: Open your eyes!

Lift them to morning light on a fragrant pasture.

Feel inspired, with senses tingling,

In the pleasure of happy experience

And a bright awakening on a new plane.

SOME POEMS

by

WINSTON MATTHEWS

Winston Matthews, a long-term cannabis activist pushing for the common use of the entire plant, likes highlighting the propaganda about it by trying to increase awareness of the benefits of cannabis and injustice of UK law. Winston stood for Parliament for the Legalise Cannabis Alliance in 2005. He worked with the cannabis consumers movement for Human rights issues. In 2012, he was incarcerated for his political believe sand his refusal to stop growing and using cannabis. Prison made him exceptionally ill but, after his release, he continued to fight for cannabis and the right to grow it at home. Winston worked with one of the main founders of Green Pride in Brighton and Worthing Coffeeshops owner, Chris Baldwin (RIP), a full-time cannabis activist who fought on bravely until his death in 2016.

NIGEL

Alcohol turns my neighbour Nigel into a mule
The fool on the fuel he thinks it's cool
Drinking in the morning Alcohol dependent
Disabled benefits to stay in his merriment!

Local landlord cant cope with him, so where hence!
Nigel goes shopping now down the off license!
The shopkeeper is allowed to say he's had enough
And Nigel knows, when he's had to bluff his stuff!

Ageing hasn't had work in years,
known as the man could hold his beers
Now as he staggers in-front of his pier
He shouts legally, lets have three cheers.

The local ambulance brought Nigel home
Collapsed on the street so he wont moan!
I told Nigel I'd write about him,
And I've tried not to make it grim.

So this chap is mentally on his knees.
I know now its part of his disease!
Socially injected with the right etiquette
And all Nigel wants to do is forget!

So poor Nigel his liver ain't happy I said!
Yet in his heart the right place he's sapid!
Yet his brains are leaving him rapid!
And the memories of sadness easily shed!

What perpetual depression
Fuel by a nightmare recession
In-turned aggression!
Nigel having another session!

MP'S OUTING TO THE SUPERMARKET TODAY! WHAT MORE CAN I SAY?

Taking the starving through the food aisles,
but don't let them eat!
Explain the reasons for our plastic smiles,
and why they need to feel defeat!
Tell them what they cannot afford the buys
Keep them fearful, just ignore the cries!

Don't listen to the need for education
As you can charge more, to learn the situation.
Don't relate,
As the starving stands at the gate! Don't think!
You'll remember the stink!

No don't worry about the smell!
The deodorant department profits will swell!
Sales will disappear through the roof!
And we get fiscal truth!

Look after that oil pipe line!
Then the world will be fine!
MP's in an expenses decline!
Whilst I think! swindling swine!

No don't worry about the tools!
We don't know better, us fools.
The armour just ain't quite right!
A small disadvantage in this fight!

Whoops the supplies are on hold
So our young troops, feel left in the cold.
Do worry, said an MP we won't gloat
By the way, can I clean my moat?

Oh yes I say sarcastically!
Cleaning equipment, is next to the pharmacy!
Just ignore the patients, waiting to be pain free!
Do I as a simpleton have to type for infinitely!
Finally! Let the monkey's read the reality!

Ignore me my medication is illegal you see.
So is my recreational substance illegal for thee!
And my attunement to spirituality!
But don't worry one day I'll be free!
To treat my pain as I see!

Ah special offers near the till
MP's have had there fill
Duty free liquid drugs
Equals insensitive immoral thugs!

You see I believe!
We are what we take!
And they are taking it all!
For goodness sake!

HUMAN RIGHTS AND HUMAN WRONGS

I'm Locked away in my cell again.
Listening to nothing,
Just the boring rain.
They are allowed to take everything that I own,
But not my dreams, as they are mine alone.

I lay awake and I think how it used to be.
Will it ever change, then I regain some sanity?
I've been incarcerated for herb growing,
Now they've stole my liberty.
Then with a slight yawn, I fall asleep

And dream that I'm not locked away any more.
Dreaming of being healthy, not wealthy
and in those dreams I saw.
Then I wake up with the noise of those heartless keys.
Opening that selfish door.

How it hurts to open your eyes, find you were only dreaming.
You wake and stare around, and you feel like screaming.
Yet... the time goes slowly,
but surely bye. then you can do, is dream!
Yes dream and cry.

SOME POEMS

By

SARAH DOUGAN
AKA SARAH SATIVA

Sarah Dougan AKA Sarah Sativa is a cannabis advocate. She has a degree in biology, has researched into cannabis for medicinal use and freely shares her knowledge with other people. Sarah runs a Facebook page called Sarah Sativa and has a web site of the same name. She has guided countless people through the use of cannabis safely. Also she has participated in many radio shows also to highlight the benefits of cannabis and have been a prominent member of many cannabis community organisations over the years.

http://www.sarahsativa.com/

PEOPLE ARE SCARED TO PLANT A SEED

They are scared to buy
What they need to grow a seed.
Once this seed has reached maturity it has amazing capabilities.
It has the potential to kill cancer cells,
Ease the symptoms of MS,
Stop pain,
Regulate hormones, temperature, alkalinity.
Strange then really, don't you think
As it can stop children having seizures,
It can stop the tremors of Parkinson's,
Ease Tourette's.
You would think everyone was going out and getting one of these seeds,
Making sure it had enough light and enough dark,
That it was warm and well watered
The air flow around it was so good so it could breath well, and help prevent it from disease.

But instead people are too scared to plant the seed
What they are scared of,
More then any disease,
Is to have their door kicked down,
To have their children taken away,
To be locked up in prison unable to work again,
The shame of being caught with that plant,
That beautiful life giving plant.
The prohibition of cannabis is a symptom of the disease of this planet.
It's up to us to plant the treatment to end the fear,
Go get them seeds plant them where they are needed,
Don't let the fear prevent you,
Don't wait for permission to have a better life.

WHAT HAS THE WORLD COME TO

What's the world come to?
It's not about love, tolerance and compassion.
The ones in so-called charge
Are causing poverty,
Are causing destruction,
Are causing blame,
Are causing infighting.
People are up in arms.
But what about?
What's being done for our starving children?
The ones criminalized for having compassion,
The big bullies running the country,
Getting everyone fighting,
Prosecuting people for cannabis
While being the world's biggest exporters,
Denying people access, to a plant which can ease so much pain,
Gives quality of life!
Yet they do sell it daily.
They say it's legal for medical use,
Yet give it to practically none.
A whole industry run underground
By good and bad people.
People with cancer, growing their own,
Scared the door will come through
What for?
Why is this a bad thing to do?
What has to happen before they let go?

They have no control
Over this.
Too many are awake
To the benefits of this plant.
Once they remove one, another plant is grown.
There are stories nearly every day in the media
About the benefits of this plant,
Yet, still, you can have your kids removed,
You can be fined,
You can go to prison,
Over 90 years after prohibition.
This plant is more used than ever
By the police with sick children,
By people with cancer,
Those struggling with arthritis,
They take the risk every day,
As the government makes millions.
The people know more than the experts
From the practical use every day.
Yes more research is needed,
Yes more regulation,
But no not more prosecution.

LOOKING INTO A CHILD'S EYES

When I look into the child's eyes
I can see the love,
I can see the fear,
I can see the sadness,
I can see the pain.
I have to explain
As too why
The only medicine that will help that child
Is not available to them.

I have to stand back
And watch
As the disease takes hold.
I have to explain
That the government is playing a game;
That game is the same
As the child plays
With her brothers and sisters
Her friends.

They are playing dress-up,
Let's pretend
That cannabis
Has no medicinal use,
That it's harmful,
That it causes mental health problems.
That it destroys communities.
We have to pretend
That its not really them doing these things.

Then we repeatedly ask
For permission,
Even though we know its a game.
We play along,
We join in.
I watch the life
Slowly ebb away,
The child can't make sense of it
As their body is dying.

They can't get it.
Over and over again,
Around in loops.
Why are the adults playing?
Why are they playing dress up
While I'm dying?
They are playing games.
My Mum and Dad.
They are also dying

They are being forced to be
A criminal,
To break the law,
Just to give one chance,
One chance to live,
One chance to be free,
Free from the pain,
Free from fear,
Free from sickness.

Free from this disease
Which has
Taken over
Our society

Which is eating them up
From inside.
Please can I be given
The opportunity
To live?

To live a life
Free from
Lies,
Games,
Replace it
With honesty,
With love,
With happiness.

With my medicine,
Is all the child asks.
This is our right as a human
To improve
Our standard of living,
To improve our quality of life.
How can I explain
To the dying child?

I write this in memory of all the beautiful children who are no longer with us. RIP beautiful angels.

TO HAVE THE EYES AND MIND OF REASON

To have the eyes and mind of reason
When all around is attacking
Misrepresenting twisting and fearful
It's the easiest place to be
Cuts through the drama
Cuts through the pain
The eyes and mind of reason
Doesn't have to jump on and off any bandwagons
It walks its own path
Keeps calm and centred
Even when under attack
By those full of fear
Mindlessly pointing and blaming
Feeling the fear
Flight or fight
Me, I will stay here
Centred in my knowing
They may come
They may try and bully
They may try fill me with fear
Poke me to fight
Poke me to flight
But I know my destiny
I know my strength and conviction
I know with an open heart
More people can hear and feel
What is real
You come for friends for family
Just makes me more determined
To stand in truth
To break the cycles of harm
I will keep going
I will keep love in my heart

SOME POEMS

By

ROCKY
VAN DE
BENDERSKUM

Ex-tramp, Ex-teacher, Ex-tremely inappropriate Too Punk to Funk, Leukaemia Survivor, my body is broken but my spirit is strong.
Scribbler of scribbles and writer of well... blah, blah, blah to be fair Anarchist Geriactivist who stood for parliament for the Legalise Cannabis Alliance in Canterbury in 2005.

http://www.benderskum.rocks

CRUMBS

Early on Sunday, I woke in my car
Easy to walk to in the dark, not too far
There you were asleep in the open
I let you be, my heart still hoping
That although it was feeling quite wrong
With a hint of atonement we'd still get along
I went to collect my things for the day
But the cookies were smashed to my dismay
Not just one or two, my thoughts were hushed
Smashed into crumbs broken crushed
But all five packets crushed to pieces
That moment the love in me simply ceases
So my cookies talk was doomed from the start
The Melon was fine but it was only a part
So when you came to talk with me with
venom in your tone
You didn't touch any part of me that bird had
already flown
I hope we can move on in time as slightly
tattered friends
I'm sad you broke my love for you that I
don't believe will mend

HISTORY, HERSTORY, OURSTORY

I'm here to tell you a story in my classical poetry style

About some prohibitionists all of whom I think were vile

Although classical style is a stretch of reality as you will quickly see

But the second line is the honest truth I'm sure you will agree

It started with a politician name of William Hearst

Eventually joined by others but he was really the first

He owned a lot of newspapers and forests to make paper with

He appeared as an honest businessman but acted like a spiv

He invented yellow journalism to make his papers sell

So instead of news there was fiction and it made the president yell

'When I open up my paper to read all of the news

I want to read the facts of it not some journalistic views'

The president's name was Theodore he invented National Parks

Lots of the land owned by William Hearst, Ted's bite was as bad as his bark

So Hearst could not cut trees down to run his paper mills

So he looked to his land in Mexico which was part of America still

So off he went to cut down trees with his usual ornery gang

But they were stopped by Pancho Villa's crew and thwarted in their plan

Mexico at this time was annexed but negotiating independence

And its president had pardoned all bandits to give himself ascendence

Pancho Villa's bandit gang had joined the northern division

Their battle song La Cucaracha caused Hearst's men indecision

They sang of Marijuana of which Hearst's men had never heard

So Hearst vilified Marijuana and Mexicans to which other racists concurred

This went on for twenty years until he joined up with some others

Many it seemed had similar views about our brown skinned brothers

Andrew Mellon oft overlooked was the US Treasury Secretary of state

His banks were invested in fossil views so hemp was something to hate

He made his niece's husband head of the Federal Bureau of Narcotics

A racist guy named Anslinger who claimed marijuana made people psychotic

He then employed a specialist Doctor James Munch

A man who was to put it plainly, was clearly out to lunch

He claimed in court and this is a fact

Smoking Marijuana turned him into a bat

Mellon teamed up with Lammot DuPont who also owned General Motors

And John D Rockefeller and some other fossil oil promoters

Between them they made growing far too expensive for even the richest hemp farmer

The Rockefeller's had all the herbalist closed down in favour of their modern Pharma

With the Marijuana Tax act firmly entrenched in the law

They lobbied the world to follow their path but greed was what it was for

Over the years activists have tried to make governments to see their mistake

But here in the UK it seems obvious to me why the initiative is so hard to take

Those here invested in the cannabis industry

Would lose a lot of profit if they make our actions free

So what is the hold up and who is to blame?

Corporations or Government, or are they one and the same?

"Choices"

STOP, GET THE FUCK OUT OF YOUR CAR, TAKE OFF YOUR SHOES AND WALK ON THE LAND

The hard times are coming it's hard to deny
Look at the climate look at the sky
Eventually they'll cut down most of the trees
And the ones that are left will be full of disease

Thousands of species go extinct every year
But the average citizen still don't care
There'll be Flora museums and Fauna zoos
When the natural has gone and nothings renewed

With their GM seeds they'll try to grow food
But with GM seeds plantings too crude
Those seeds need the chemicals made out of oil
They were never designed to grow just in soil

There'll soon be no oil for plastic or cars
Unless they discover a supply on Mars
With the air too polluted and food really short
They'll look to the pasts ignored lessons taught

By then it's too late and there's no turning back
Too late to fix it or pick up the slack
There will still be roads from this place to that
But no life in sight not even a cat

THE DREAM

Dark, Dystopian, Dysfunctional Days
Nobody is free, everyone pays
The days are scary even though it is light
But when it grows dark in comes the night
Restless night crazy dreams
Nothing really what it seems
It all begins with a fire in the woods
With best friend on guard sleep if you could
But the night is dark and full of scares
To catch you if you're unawares
The eyes have it, the eyes to the right
But they cannot see on this moonless night
The private detective gives them a clue
Then, in they charge straight for you
A golf-playing judge hitch-hikes to the coast
Away from the forest and the red cloaked ghost
Victory signs the protest marcher
Caught in the gaze of an eyeless archer
Whether he's an archer or merely a bowman
Hanging a scarecrow is a very bad omen
The popo move forward still aided by the sleuth
And a painter in a waterfall is painting the truth
While every moment facing his fears
Of death by drowning in a Big Wave of tears
Whatever label they give you be it Activist, Tramp or Bum
Sleep soundly, weary travelling man, for tomorrow never comes

COAST

LIZARD THOUGHTS

We are watching you there in your halls of
splendour waiting to glimpse your hidden
agenda

We've seen all the signs, watched all the
news! Nothing you say will change our views

We see all your fake needed budget cuts you
think you just can, cos we haven't the guts

But be wary we have become many somehow
you seem to be affecting everyone now

As for everyone it gets rougher
But first the vulnerable have to suffer

GOING, GOING, GONE.

When he wrote in his book, he wanted you to look.
He wanted you to stare at what he wrote there.
He wanted to share to see that you care.
He laid himself bare too late to repair.
He laid himself bare but you still didn't care.
Now he wants you to feel as he winds in the reel
That this isn't a dream it's really quite real.
He once spouted love like a babbling brook
Now he wants you to look,,
As you're stuck on his hook.
So now you're in pain and it's not quite the same..
Your eyes fill with tears, this isn't a game.
It was him you framed, it was him you blamed
With your spiteful words it was him that you shamed.
You can scream out in fear but there's no-one to hear,
As he gives you a smile without any cheer.
You know it's too late as he fastens the gate
When you look in his eyes and only see hate.
He has seen through your lies no farewells no goodbyes,
Just a halo of flies.
It's the night of your death
So take your last breath.

WEIRD WORLD

The sky went weird the people feared but the
wind blew hard and then it cleared
The sky turned blue and clear and true in the
aftermath there was much to do
But that leaves nothing for the papers to say
it's just a very ordinary day
It is hard to see beyond the disguise that they
hide behind to make us despise
The bombs are dropped and a country cries
So they don't tell the truth it's always lies but
because of their actions the children still die
An eye for an eye and tooth for a tooth more
lies the wars are for oil and that's the truth
It's what they do it's up to you, to believe
what they say or see right through
Then put them to shame for them it's a game
to make the world appear insane
So remember this and never forget for the
good in us all is not gone yet
While walking through a world of treacle,
you'll meet a lot of sticky people

THERE'S DARKNESS INSIDE

I'd like to inform you I'm not really nice
and if you could see it I know you'd think twice
I try to be cheerful I try to be glad
but there's darkness inside that makes me quite mad
The facts are plain and I don't try to hide
if you look past the smile there's darkness inside

You can't really tell what's lurking deep down always
a smile, the man about town
But catch me off guard and look really hard
gaze at my core all bitter and chard
The facts are plain and I don't try to hide
if you look past the smile there's darkness inside

I seem to be happy and always to smile
but look inside and you'd run a mile
I'm not talking hurt I'm not talking pain
I'm talking of darkness buried deep in my brain
The facts are plain and I don't try to hide
if you look past the smile there's darkness inside

You'd not send me messages or texts on the phone
you'd keep well away and leave me alone
If you look past the smile you will see what I mean
there's darkness inside its plain to be seen
The facts are plain and I don't try to hide
if you look past the smile there's darkness inside

STOCKHOLM SYNDROME

I remember the first time that we met
You were nice and seemed a safe bet
I was lost but I felt I had been found
You made me stop and turn my life around

But once your feet were under the table
I saw the bitter truth behind your oh so sweet label
You weren't the person I thought I knew but a complete and utter stranger
I used to think that we were safe tii you put my life in danger

Your words of love were only lies and hollow
But as your prisoner of your lies I continued to follow
My body and my mind had never been so bruised
Is this Stockholm syndrome or am I just confused?

Thought you were my lover but you turned into a hater
My wounds became deeper than the deepest crater

KNOW YOUR ROOTS

Wednesday
We all arrive to form our crew
Everyone wondering what to do
Come time to eat, we all ate Nasi
Common or garden nothing snazzy
Got a little bolloxed on some very tasty medibles
Wandered to the fire the cannafam incredibles
Did I really say that or did I merely think it?
Careful with that bong water, oh no please don't drink it
Then off to bed for a well earned rest
My cannafam tribe are proper the best

Thursday
Woke in the daylight but still not too early
Very gently no hurly burly
Coffee, Tea, Wake and Bake time
Then more preparation it'll all work out fine
Climbing on tables, while they're strimming the grass
Careful not to fall on your arse
Everyone's buckets cough, cough, cough
I never got on so I'm not falling off
Trolley that is same one as you
The dabber was slow but will definitely do
They say he's a rare kid but he looks just the same
With a dab and a bucket he's definitely to blame
Cough, cough, cough because of a bong
I'm pretty sure another will soon be along
Buncha hippies sitting round the fires glow
Talking about the sorta stuff most of we already know

The energy of this cannafam is a power that needs a looking
Joints abound, joints around and this all after cooking
Another night of smoke and munch
For this very special lovely bunch

Friday
A Callie clipper sticker to start another day
But absolutely nowhere to spend my undercover pay
Hanging around leaning on a bow a bit like Robin Hood
Gutting rabbits talk on a vegan festy didn't seem so good
With a mega lung to mention
Much more a thing than mere suggestion
With a lung and a lung and a lung another day of wakey-bakey fun
I need a cup of tea and probably many more than one
A little while later the doughnut eaters arrive
Quick, duck, run away, everybody hide
Bales of hay are sorted and leaflets folded too
But hair cooked in chocolate is what I'd call Eeuw
28.8.06 is what I think it said
The number that are printed on the back of that young man's head
The sun was as hot as fuck right then so we hid in the marquee shade instead
The banner in the wind needed constant re-adjustment
And the cannaflag was flying if only for a moment
There were mad, mad herbs consumed that afternoon
Stick your fingers in its bum she said, is it too early is it too soon?
Time to have another lung but this time it is live

This weekend is really smoking I only hope my lungs survive
Live stream chats with cough, cough, choke
With Pinky and some of those proper clever blokes
The clever young man with the numbers was worried about the streams
Amid babble over easy and countless woken pipe dreams
My lungs had now been opened but whodafuckingthunkit?
And not a single sound from the hippy with his drumkit
Fresh as a mushy that could have come all the way from Mexico
The world was burped up backwards so that was the time to pack and go

Saturday
Wake and bake with body ache
This tiny puddle will soon be a lake
Busy, busy stall to prepare
I worry about the state of my hair
Another list is scribbled out
Microphone wafty? Don't worry I'll shout
Sativa said she'd start her talk
In her spanking new T-shirt then walk the walk
Chat, chat, chat, I will represent
One love for cannabis is what I think she meant
Simpa on a microbe phone came across real smooth
Knows his stuff that young man does and tells the proper truze
Then it was the time for the cannabis clubs
Telling of better recreation than in pubs

The cannafam is growing from this to me is clear
Time to educate the masses and extinguish their age old fear
The cannafam continued late into the night
Talking over this and that putting the world to rights
I went to make some scran cos starveling was my mode
But everything had turned to shit ready to explode

Sunday

When I wake I'm in my car, numb legs, hands and feet
But the every present smile on my face is very hard to beat
Got shouted at some more today
But no my smile is here to stay
A little bit of rain well that just can't be bad
Which quickly turned to sunshine and made the people glad
While reversing a scooter there was almost a tragedy
The cake stand saved by Callum definitely a hero he
All a bit slower everyone tired but the day moves on
And the little baby plants are ready to be gone
A whole lot more of the blah, blah, blah
Spliffs, lungs and bongs how bizarre
For me I mean as I just don't smoke
But after the lungs it was toke, toke, toke
When it was done and dusted the marquee was taken down
Many folks were leaving this little eco town

SIXTH MASS EXTINCTION

There are holes in the sky where radiation gets in
But these holes are huge and will burn your skin
With a planet that's dying its long time for change
Or just try to ignore me and think that I'm strange
Moan about delays caused by planet protectors
And soon our world will be just full of spectres
I hope the word change will enter your head
For nothing can live on a world that is dead
You may do your recycling and think it's enough
But the world is a candle about to be snuffed
It's not quite too late there's still stuff we can do
But that includes everyone, you, you and you
We need an end to the corporate greed
And stop keep on buying all that shit you don't need
When the air is polluted and the water is too
The only wild animals will be soon in a zoo
Species are dying not just names on a list
Doesn't that make you shake your fist?

In the sixties they told us this was to come
But they were ignored so nothing was done
There are still people saying that it's just not the truth
While ignoring the facts and blind to the proof
When the government forms a department of death
Remember my words as we take our last breath

TICK TOCK, TICK TOCK

Whatever happ'ed to my wings said the Kentucky fried bird
Very, very quietly but everybody heard
I don't have arms so I don't need sleeves
And I'm not a cup of tea as I don't have leaves
I bet you can imagine if you think real hard
I'm just a stolen tenner from a birthday card
This might just be some words a load of nonsense, Babble
But every single letter here is in your game of scrabble
As I was walking up the stairs eating a plate of frozen soya
I spy with my little eye a painting made by Francisco Goya
It was called Two Old Ones Eating Soup
Painted on the walls before he flew the coop
With the tick-less version of a cuckoo clock
Although you listen really hard you will only hear a tock

GOODNIGHTS TO HUMAN RIGHTS

Animals it seems feel no pain
unless they live in France or Spain

Or anywhere else that isn't insane
but in Britain the animals feel no pain

If you think that's a joke there's worse to come
your rights eroded by political scum

Ignore what is said behind their sales pitches
and they'll do what they like without any hitches

Their salesman tells you when it's gone it's gone
and there go your rights one by one

Hark at the sounds of insidious laughter
a feudal system is what they're after

They really don't listen to me or you
they were voted in and they'll do what they do

Back to the animals who they say feel no pain
They consider us animals we're one and the same.

SOME POETRY

by

PHIL MONK

Phil Monk, erstwhile teacher of four subjects, disabled by chronic myofascial pain from joint hypermobility spectrum disorder, arthritis, depression and PTSD, now Human Rights Cannabis Activist and founder of We The Undersigned Have a Human Sovereign Right to Cannabis (WTU).
Phil says
"I learned the truth about cannabis, prohibition, how long the UK Government has known the truth, suppressed it and misinformed the public, destroying millions of lives by prosecution, whilst capitalising and monopolising the therapeutic benefits they refused to recognise."

https://www.wtuhq.org/

I WISH I'D STUDIED LAW

There are few perks to being chronically Ill.
Definitely not the side effect ridden pill
Muscles hurt so lying still
Listening in dread for the Old Bill

Lying awake from pain induced insomnia
Remembering my studies and academia
This allows one quiet time to ponder
For mind to drift, wander and wonder

The pain and misery that has been caused
By deceitful policies which are greatly flawed
Driven by ideology, racism and greed
Imprisoning and fining us for planting seed

Profiting from our so called criminality
Reveals the depths of their immorality
Denying our CannaFolks access to herbal vitality
Recognised and utilised for millennia by humanity

Until lies, greed and corruption
Created almighty confusion
Through government misinformation
To deliberately fool our once trusting Nation

Question is what will you do?
Keep ya head down till they come for you?
Or will you stand for truth?
And demand from them burden of proof?

That cannabis holds such deadly potential harm
That we poor commoners must be forbidden to farm

Yet what is this hypocritical nonsense?
Wealthy corporations can pay for a licence!

To Cultivate these 'dangerous drugs'
To sell overseas but not to us mugs!
There's far more honour among the thugs
Where we usually go to find our frosty nugs!

Their cannabis derived products make people choke
Charging sick people who are broke
Saying cannabis grown by CannaFolk
Is dangerous, but what a ridiculous joke!

We care for our plants as they care for us
With maximum love and minimum fuss

So I'm trying to learn all I see and hear
That no more CannaFam lives in fear
Can live in peace with those you hold dear
No Keeping awake to make sure you can hear

For that dreaded boot through the door!

Shame I trained to be a teacher,
Wish I'd studied law!

STILL IN BED FEELING TIRED AND BROKEN

Still in bed feeling tired and broken
Both in soul, body and mind
After KyR where all was spoken
But new levels of pain
I did find Such levels of pain and disability
Made me want to discontinue
My existence in this reality
To unburden my lovely Lou
My body is still in recovery
Muscles torn and sinews afraid
Mind struggling to climb from this misery
A lifetime of this pain makes me afraid
Every movement causes burning pain
Starting to drive me a little insane
Feeling like limbs of lead,
Joints of crushed glass.
Barbed wire for muscle and sinew
Perished bands for tendons and ligaments
Chronic myofascial pain from joint hypermobility
spectrum disorder
Really is no fun
Definitely no day out in the sun.
But I have never been a quitter
Which stems from when I was fitter
And means I have made up my mind
Against the act of suicide It pains and grieves my soul
The Injustice that the authorities
Prosecutes you for feeling whole

Through herbal cannabis health remedies
Bad enough I must fight this condition
Made worse for fighting against
Blatant greed and corruption
By those proclaiming to be saints
So soon I will be back in the saddle
Once my body has recovered
Making the case to challenge their twaddle
With many documents I've uncovered

Printed in Poland
by Amazon Fulfillment
Poland Sp. z o.o., Wrocław